I0684510

Memory of Desire

Sexy Stories Collection

VOLUME 28

12 EROTIC SHORT STORIES

JULLES MUNSEN

BLANCA CRANSTON

Publisher's Note: This is a work of fiction. Names,
characters, places, and incidents are a product of
the author's imagination. Locales and public
names are sometimes used for atmospheric
purposes. Any resemblance to actual people, living
or dead, or to businesses, companies, events,
institutions, or locales is completely coincidental.

Memory of Desire/ Julles Munsen, Blanca
Cranston. -- 1st ed.
Xplicit Press, an imprint of TLM Media LLC

ISBN-13: 978-1-62327-559-4
ISBN-10: 1-62327-559-8
eISBN: 978-1-62327-609-6

Printed in the United States of America

CONTENTS

1 BURNING DESIRE

Tammy looked out of the car window. The car was going too fast for her to make out anything of the passing scene outside. Her mind was as blurred as the view. Many thoughts jumbled up and created chaos. She shook her head as if to brush away these thoughts. She leaned back on the seat and tried to sleep. Her hand moved over her panties under the short dress.

Tammy had always been a bit on the wilder edge of life. She had been a promiscuous child, always liking the skin contact, the hugs, and the kisses people showered on her. Whenever some outsider picked up to kiss her, she would always move her face to let her lips touch the kisser's. She got a thrill playing naked in the bathtub and enjoyed the maid scrubbing her all over with her rough hands. She had started masturbating at the age of 11 or 12, when she hardly even understood what she was doing to herself.

It was no surprise that she grew up to be an even more promiscuous adult. She was a beautiful young girl. Her slender waist stood out from her heavy breasts and arched out hips, giving her figure an hourglass look. She wore revealing clothes and enjoyed attention she got from males of all age groups. Her pussy always burned and itched for a touch. She was passion incarnated and was never satisfied. She was always horny, always yearning for some kind of sexual gratification. Her carnal impulses and desires were also not the familiar ordinary ones. If she could not find a lover, she got something else from a vibrator to a wooden stick or even her pet dogs have licked her to satisfaction.

She returned home after spending a weekend with Steven. She had met him at a common friend's home, and her former lover Bryan had introduced them. The weekend was lovely but too short for Tammy. Steven was pretty good as far as Friday night and whole of Saturday. But Tammy found him difficult and tired most of Sunday. So they are returned back early to the town.

Tammy closed her eyes and thought of the lovely Saturday night. They had stayed almost naked after reaching the hotel on Friday night, and Steven was obsessed with her beautiful body. Her milky white tits were huge and the pink nipples erect and inviting.

"Oh god! Ohhhhhhhh...honey I am coming," Tammy had screamed as she dug her nails in his bare back. She begged him to go faster and not stop. Steve increased his fucking speed, pounding faster with each whack and trying to drive his hard cock all the way through the hot hungry bitch lying under him. He marveled at such a phenomenal sexual hunger Tammy was displaying! He had known Tammy for only two weeks, and by this time, she was already fucking him to death!

Tammy was a woman with more sexual energy than most men. That's why Bryan never once hesitated when Steven showed interest in taking her out. Steven now realized Bryan was trying to get out of a demanding state of affairs he was unable to handle. Initially, everything was wonderful for Steven. This 23-year-old busty woman let him do whatever and whenever he wanted to her. He made love to her in all possible positions and most possible places—even once out in the public view. She was a lover's delight. But her only problem was that her sexual frenzy began to start only when her mate was already famished. She had sucked Steven dry and still wanted more. On his last day, while travelling back, Steven tried to think of a friend or colleague or even his own boss to whom he could pass on this sex maniac. But presently, he had to concentrate on the seductress trying to end him totally with her demands. As soon as he came with a force and rolled on his side to have some rest, her hand again started to move over his aching tired cock. She tried to pull him over her pussy and asked him to lick her once more. "Please Steven, it feels so good when you move your tongue over my hairless love triangle." He stayed inert and started at the roof. God! He thought, she needs more than a single man for one session. One man can never fulfill her hungers. She then put his idle hand over her taut nipples and moved it over her boobs. Steven failed to turn on. He was so tired after a two-day hectic sex schedule. "I am no machine Tam, please let me have some rest!" he tried to sound gentle but could not hide the edge from his voice. He wished to move his hand up her neck and throttle it. He was shocked when he saw that after his clear refusal, Tammy started to rub her own hand over her swollen clit. She was soon moaning softly, her eyes closed and chest heaving up and down.

She was no less than a magical wet and hot dream available in flesh. Her ass started to grind in sync with her hand movements, and Steven could see wetness oozing out from her love hole. Her excited body tightened due to sexual agitation, and she looked like a fair-skinned Barbie doll with beautiful blond hair and shapely figure. She was indeed a doll with a never-failing battery, though she seemed to have lost her off button.

Steven got up and moved to the shower, while Tammy climaxed herself to a body shaking orgasm.

They had not talked after his refusal. She had this overwhelming need to cum every couple of hours and that was too much for Steven.

Tammy was thinking of a way already to get relief to her rising urges. It was quite apparent to her that she wouldn't be getting that relief from Steven. They hired the cab on Steven's name. She stared at the young driver. She moved her tongue on her lips as the young cabby looked at her staring at him in the rear view mirror. It was hard to escape the fire in her eyes. He blushed at the way she openly stared and started to get a nice feeling in his groin. He could see her huge tits peeping out of her low-cut neckline. He could also see the thirst in her eyes, thirst for some male juices. What he wasn't aware was how tough it was to quench her thirst.

He was going to be the next passenger on her journey of passionate love pursuits. The pursuits that burnt many. She asked the driver to drop Steven first. When they reached Tammy's home, it was already midnight. She got down from the car and went towards the driver's seat. "You are cute!" she purred. He smiled and stared at her tits popping out of her satin blouse as she bent down through his window. "Come in and I will show where these end," she pointed to her tits and beckoned him to follow him. He hurriedly parked the car. His hands shook at the thought of his good luck at being able to fuck such a gorgeous lady. He followed her in like a little puppy at heels of his mistress.

As soon as he was inside her home, Tammy ran a hot bath. She felt quite mucky after two days of hot sweaty sex with Steven. Now, she needed a nice hot bath to relax her before she made use of the young man in her room. She beckoned him in the bathroom and was already naked as he entered. She admired her nude image in the full-length mirror on the door's back. As she stepped into the bubble bath, she patted its edge and asked the cabby to sit on it. He removed his clothes, put them in a neat pile on a sideboard, and sat down on edge of bathtub his legs hanging in the water. He admired the woman in front of him displaying the ultimate glory of physical charm with even firm skin, supple body, full firm breasts, blue eyes, blonde hair, long shapely limbs; it was the kind of body any man would love to kill for!

Looking at the unknown stranger, Tammy cupped her full tits and showed him her nipples getting stiff. He moved his hand to them to stroke them. She then pulled him in the water and pulled his hand over her stiff and puffy pussy, which was still tingling from the use by Steven's big cock. But as his hand touched the swollen pussy, it started to exude wetness again. She breathed hard at the thought of another cock filling her love hole. That is the best sensation any women could ever get, she thought. She, if she got her way, would never let her pussy go empty even for a minute.

Their nude bodies slid over each other in the warm water. Tammy felt her tired muscles opening up and relaxing under the effect of balmy water combined with gentle touches of her partner. They made love for almost an hour, slowly, gently, a sensual feeling flowed in their bodies and a sexy fragrance of their combined juices filled the bathroom. The other thing that filled the house was low soft moaning sounds from Tammy, which made the young man mad with passion.

Getting out of the bath, they walked naked into the bedroom and the young man lay down on the soft bed in a relaxing posture. Tammy jumped over him and started to rub her wet body over his. He was on again and was pumping her pussy hole with new fervor in less than 10 minutes. He simply loved this wild cat he had laid his hands upon.

They made love over and over again, throughout the day. Soon, the cabby started to get tired and felt like running away from the "possessed" lady. She was so hungry; his cock ached with being abused for 4–5 hours. He made his escape as Tammy dozed off, stretched naked on the bed. Her hand was still on her pussy.

Tammy kept hooking known-unknown hot men to quench her never-satiating thirst and always ended up making these men loathe sex for many days after a tiring, wild stint with her!

It had been almost a week since Tammy had had sex. She was hungry that day, sexually hungry, as she entered the cabin of her boss, Daniel. Without wasting time, Tammy started to move her skirt up. He had heard of Tammy's escapades but never thought he would have a chance to taste this wild ripe fruit. He beamed as Tammy slowly undressed to reveal her black lingerie. He watched her and marveled at the body of the full sensuous young blonde. One look at her pussy told him that she was hungry. "Ahhhh...," he sighed at the sight of the smooth lipped cunt. Tammy looked him in the eye and said, "Follow me," and lead Daniel to the couch placed at a corner of the office. She poured wine for both of them and asked him to get rid of his clothes so that they could do some serious work!

Tammy reclined on the couch and spread her legs wide. Her smooth, shaven sex mound was exposed in an astonishingly vulgar way. Without waiting for his response, she poked her fingers into her pussy and softly started to masturbate. Daniel stood silently, as if mesmerized, while Tammy's fingers shot in and out of her salivating slit. Her other hand moved to her chest, kneading and cupping her full breasts. The sound of her heavy breathing filled the room. Daniel couldn't stand it any longer. He quickly moved over her and started to lick her drooling pussy. She grabbed his hard on and sucked it gently. They both worked with their tongues over each other's genitals and the speed of their movements increased gradually. Daniel's fat cock was glistening with precum and saliva now. He lay down over Tammy and fucked her missionary style. He was almost double her age and was super excited to fuck a hot young girl right in his office. He pumped her hard and worked to a climax. Tammy was moaning loudly. They locked eyes, gyrating together in throes of frenzied passion; Daniel sensed her cunt muscles start to contract, indicating that her pussy was going to lose hold and have an orgasm. Daniel's cock jerked hard as his orgasm ripped through the head of his pulsating tip, while Tammy's climax made her tight ass bounce up and down on the couch until the blissful moment passed.

Tammy smiled a flirtatious smile, reached under the beer belly of Daniel and again grabbed his slack cock. With the other hand, she again audaciously fingered her vagina.

She rubbed her young body with the plump soft body of Daniel. He was different from other men she had taken, like a ripe fruit full of pulp and juices. Once she got her pussy wet again, she was hard to stop. She pushed one of her tits in Daniel's mouth, and he started to suck obediently. He was still gripping with the after effects of his recent orgasm, as Tammy pumped his cock with her hand to make it hard again. She then placed his manhood over her damp pussy, inside her lips bulging with sexual tension and pushed it inside her dewy slit glistening with her own juices. She pushed his hips into motion and helped him to dig deeper in her. Daniel soon got active again and the head of his thick cock inched its way into Tammy's slippery pussy. He shed a huge load of cum over her belly as they orgasmed again together.

Daniel never had such a hard work out with any other woman so far. After having a spectacle of the erotic side of Tammy, he helped her a couple times a week to put out the rampant fire in Tammy's loins.

Tammy's obsession with older men followed with boys as young as 18–19. She charmed them with her semi-naked body as she roamed near college campuses and coffee shops.

The guys couldn't help but marvel how this attractive young blonde had become so hooked to orgasms. It didn't matter how frequently or how many times she got to fuck, it wasn't just ever completely enough to satiate her inflamed pussy.

2 OFFICIALLY AN ADULT PART 1

The Flashback

Emily, a sexy teenager, was almost always horny. She, besides her several sexual exploits, was obsessed with the desire to have sex with her childhood friend, Alexander. This is a series of two short stories about her losing her virginity to her gym coach, on an impulse, and finally, using her sexual expertise to have sex with Alexander on her 19th birthday. The sexy, bewitching, Emily is sure to become your sexual fantasy.

Monday, 9th November

Emily woke up to a lovely morning. She was feeling lovely, too. Why not! In a week's time, she was going to be 18. She was eagerly waiting for that day, marked boldly with the red pen on the calendar. She had a lot to do this week. She had to plan, shop, and arrange. It was going to be the best day of her life, she promised herself.

With such energetic thoughts, Emily climbed down from her bed. She was a beautiful 18-year-old girl with pale skin with a tint of pink, long flowing, reddish brown hair, brown doe eyes, and full luscious lips. Her young body was blossoming beautifully. The curves were all there already, but the leanness of structure was also still intact. She looked like a sexy nymph, and she was fully aware of the effect she had on boys and men. Emily enjoyed all the attention her looks fetched her.

Therefore, when Alexander showed indifference, she felt awkwardly wounded, as if she lost a game. A game where she thought she could woo any man she chose. However, Emily was not going to take this defeat as a final one. She would fight harder. Seduce Alex. If need be... beg him for sex! She had never heard of girls forcing sex on a guy.

"Do girls beg guys for sex?" She chuckled at this thought and started to get ready for another day of school.

Emily spent an extra hour in the bath, making love to herself and was, again, late for the school bus. She often got horny in the shower, as she slowly undressed. Her beautiful breasts, with delicate pink nipples, get hard as water falls on them, and turns her on. She moves her hand over her smooth skin and teases her nipples. She is always amused as to how a touch on her breasts makes her wet down between the thighs. She soaped her breasts and thighs, sexily, and her fingers slipped all over her wet, naked body. Her hand slowly moved down on her flat tummy, towards the heaven all men hungered for. She, leisurely, stroked her wet pussy and purred like a naughty kitten.

As the excitement mounted up, the stroking movement of her fingers got faster. She moaned out loud, as her fingers entered her love hole. Her pussy was dripping with her female juices, and the aroma of her wetness was stronger than the scent of the lavender soap. She stroked and poked with her finger for a long time. Her breathing was uneven and her body was shaking with excitement. Although she came in the end, she was not satisfied. She needed a man, with a hard dick to amuse her, satisfy her, and make her shout with ecstasy. She wanted

Alexander, so she had to reach school.

She was late, as usual. The fucking school bus had left, again, without her. Yet, that never bothered her much. She was popular and had loads of friends. Someone would soon come along and give her a ride to school. She hoped it was Alex. Yet, instead, Samantha pulled in and Emily, half-heartedly, hopped into her friend's car. After a quick, "Hi," Emily closed her eyes and starts to think about her favorite topic these days, "Alexander."

Alexander Brown is Emily's dad's friend's son. They have known each other since their early childhood years. As Emily grew up, prettier with each passing year, Alex, too, grew up, to be a dashing young man. He was tall, tanned, a bit muscular (enough at his age), and had a sexy mop of shining black hair, which makes him look so tempting. His only problem is that he gets too stiff around Emily. Not at the RIGHT PLACE, though! His aloofness made Emily mad, and the thought of making love with Alex started turning into an obsession. Her friends often teased her that, maybe, due to their family relations, Alex thought of her as a sister. Such thoughts pissed Emily off, badly. She wanted Alex, as a woman wants a man, to feed her hunger for love, more of a carnal nature. She wanted Alex to fuck her hard, like no man had ever done before.

Her reverie ended abruptly, as Samantha stopped the car, with a loud screech just outside the school. As she climbed out of the car, Emily smoothed her skirt over her beautiful firm ass, in full view of many senior boys. Some gasped loudly, which made Emily pep up.

"Horny bitch," smirks Samantha.

"Call me 'sex-princess,' Sam," Emily winked back at her friend, as they moved towards class.

Alex was already there, sitting right on the first bench, as usual.

"Bookworm!" Emily hissed as she passed him. He looked up at her with an angry frown, before busying himself back in his journal.

Emily's attention was not in the class. She had to plan for the next Sunday, her birthday. It was not that Emily was sex-starved. No, she was not a virgin. She had never believed in gifting her virginity to some special guy in her life. For her, sex has always been a "hunger," just like the hunger for food. Still, she wanted to be well prepared before a sex date with Alex. She remembers the various times she has had sex, in the past year after she turned 18, with various men. "Men are more fun," she mused. They are more aware of bodily needs, and they do not stumble about, like the young boys, on their first date. Her first was Andrew, her gym instructor. After one year, she still remembered that day so clearly. It was after her first fight with Alex. They were good friends, Emily and Alex, until that night, at the movies.

Emily, Alex, and a couple of other friends from school had gone to a movie. It was a romantic movie, with some brief lovemaking scenes. Eighteen-year-old Emily felt a strange awkwardness during one such scene and her hand accidentally touched Alex's. She felt her body going taut and her breathing uneven. He was also shifty, in his seat. There was an obvious physical tension between her and Alex.

Emily noticed a couple in front of them kissing and caressing each other. She moved her hand over his arm and felt him getting shaky. They both looked at each other. Emily moved her head closer to Alex and closed her eyes, and she waited for a kiss. They had kissed, earlier, but not like the hot couple on the screen. Alex, undecided for a long minute, moved his hand out from her grip and turned his face to the other side. Emily failed to understand what was happening between them. She understood the tension, a sensation of need to hold and touch, but she couldn't understand Alex's coldness. She remembered how she laid awake, all night after the movie, and wanted Alex to make tender love to her.

The next day in school, she, again, found him cold and aloof. She tried to talk about the night before, but Alex kept avoiding her. After her lots cajoling, shouting, and crying, Alex told her that he did not want any trouble in his life right now. Especially, with a rich, pampered girl. He might think about all this after she became an adult, officially. He had stressed on the word "officially," as if Emily had been secretively sleeping with all the boys around. She was already "official," she was already eighteen. More or less, they stopped meeting much after this silly incident. She hated him for rejecting her, though only for a few days. Later, she spent long moments thinking of getting that arrogant brat into her bed.

Later the same day, after school, when Emily went to gym, she was distracted and irritated. She was mad at Alex. Sensing Emily's foul temper, that day, Andrew, the gym instructor, asked her if she would like to have a coke in the gym's café, before they started with the gym routine for the day. She agreed, as she badly wanted a change of mood. They made small talk in the café, as they had diet cokes. Andrew, a muscular man, in his late twenties, was an ardent lover of pretty, rich teens, who came to him for physical training. Emily had been his favorite. He had always liked the way she dressed, so provocatively, in costly gym gear. Her tops were always the tightest and her shorts, always the shortest.

Emily noticed how Andrew's eyes lingered on her legs in the cafe. She loved attention, and this pepped her mood considerably. She tried to push Alex to a back room in her mind. She innocently placed her hand on her thigh and slowly rubbed there. Andrew stared at the milky white thighs, which were almost naked, had it not been for the tiny piece of dark blue cloth that was supposed to be a pair of gym shorts. He often noticed how her shorts habitually failed to cover up her whole firm, rounded ass, ending almost midway. Encouraged by Emily's changed mood, and her sexy body language, he stared at her tight gym shirt. She had beautifully shaped tits, as evident from her tee. If he stared hard, he could even guess the positioning of her nipples under the shirt, as she seemed to be wearing no bra underneath. Girls who do not wear underclothes are his favorite. Emily stimulated him further, as her stare followed his, and she looked down, at her tits, and smiled, shyly.

She innocently touched his hand, or arm, a number of times in the gym later. He smiled and moved closer to her. He did not stiffen like stupid Alex! They laughed a good deal that day during gym, and the innocent touches increased in frequency. She looked sexily at him, as she moved towards the showers, after the workouts. He followed, like a tamed pup. She mused, "Not all men are like Alex." She was happy that she was desirable and not some heap of rubbish, like Alex made her feel.

Emily was still peeling off her sweaty clothes, when she felt someone helping her with the shorts. She looked back, to see Andrew there. "You forgot to lock the door honey," he breathed on her neck.

"I never wanted to lock it," Emily smiled, seductively. As he undressed her, Emily felt the urgency in his moves, and hunger in his eyes, which admired her nude body. She looked down and saw a perfect hard-on under his gym pants. She moved her hand over the hardness and laughed, "What are you hiding in here?"

She'd seen porn stars mouthing something like this, often, in porn videos. Andrew laughed and, in a quick move, removed his tee and gym pants. Emily gasped out loud. She had never seen such a thing in real life. Andrew's cock was huge.

She became thrilled and alarmed, at the same time. "I'm 18, but I am still a virgin," she whispered. Her voice was like quivering honey.

He held her face, with his hands and winked, as he replied, "That's what I am an expert in, deflowering beautiful virgins." He kissed her full, sensual lips and stroked her neck, gently.

A hand moved to her bare back, gently relaxing her. She closed her eyes to control the panic, setting in, and imagined it being Alex holding her nude body. She relaxed. Andrew was truly an expert. Each touch of his hand, followed by lips and tongue, burned Emily with desire. He teased her delicate breasts with expert moves. He licked the nipples, until they grew erect and ached for more of his touch. Emily curved her back to make it easier for Andrew to reach her nipples. While his tongue worked on her tits, his hands moved back, toward her firm ass. She felt her thighs getting wetter with each move from Andrew. She realized how lovely it was to be touched by a man. Andrew slowly picked her up and placed her on the edge of the slab holding the sink.

He pushed her long, silky hair away from her body. Her body was wet with his licks and looked extremely sexy. He then moved her legs apart and moved his head forward. Emily felt a new surge of sexual flush in her body, as he touched her wet pussy with his tongue. She felt heavenly.

Andrew started to lick her pink mound of sexy flesh, which held the gateway to sexual heaven. His hands moved all over Emily's back, tits, and thighs. Her juices began to flow with some urgency. Emily looked at their reflection in the mirror, on the opposite wall, and wondered how stunning they both looked without clothes. The muscular handsomeness of Andrew's tanned, tall, and well-built body, fully complemented the delicate sensuality of her pale, thin build, with shapely limbs and curvaceous hips and breasts. Her eyes, she noticed, were burning with a wild desire. She felt as if she was made for enjoying and giving sensual pleasures.

Suddenly, Andrew lifted her legs and placed them on his shoulders. He tilted her body a bit, backwards. Her erected nipples arched forward and the tits looked like small hills. He moved forward and Emily noticed how, just like porn videos, he lubricated the tip of his dick with his spit. She felt a sensation of fear gripping her. Will she be hurt if he puts that enormous thing in? Andrew sensed her apprehension and caressed her legs, lovingly, to relax her. He started teasing her pussy with the tip of his dick. She felt herself relaxing and ready for the strike. Andrew turned on the overhead shower before he pushed his dick in, to break in the virginity of tender Emily. The water made their bodies slippery. Suddenly, a sharp pain hit Emily, and she felt as if she was going to collapse. Andrew's hand stroked her, gently, and the water falling soothingly on her started to relax her. She realized she had closed her eyes tightly and gripped Andrew on his shoulders. The dick remained inert in her for a minute, waiting for her to relax, before moving in a slow rhythm. Emily noticed the water trickling from her thighs turning red. She closed her eyes again, and concentrated on the movement of Andrew's manhood inside her. Her unease diminished, and slowly, she started to enjoy the rhythm of the pumping movements of his cock. She smiled at Andrew, and moaned, softly. He started to move faster, boosted by her leisurely moans. Emily moved her ass, in pace to his movements, and kneaded her tits. The tempo of moves and sighs increased with each passing minute. Soon, the shower reverberated with the erotic sounds. They were both panting, when Andrew came on her tummy.

Emily returned back to the present when Samantha shook her hard. School was over for the day, and Emily had not even noticed how the day went by. Her mind had been on her lovely sexual encounters, in the past.

3 OFFICIALLY AN ADULT PART 2

The Revenge

Saturday, 14th November

Emily glanced at her watch and studied her shopping list. It's perfect, she smiled. She looked stunning in her off-shoulder, lemon colored dress, which barely reached her mid thighs. It was a flowing outfit and, as she swayed, her white lace panties peeped out. She had no bra on and her tits jiggled in her thin dress as she moved. She looked every bit of SEXY. She put on her white pumps and sprayed an ample amount of her favorite body mist. "That's it," she smiled satisfactorily, after a final look at herself in the mirror.

Emily purchased all the items on her list and carefully locked them in the trunk of her car. Her next stop was Alexander's house. She had waited a year for this trip. Emily was sure to catch him alone at this time of the day, as his parents would both be away at work. She remembered how, at certain moments in last year, Alex had tried to revive their friendship. She wanted revenge, a sexual revenge!

The door was opened by a freaky-looking guy. Emily went in without waiting for a formal welcome by the weirdo. Ah! There, on the couch, was her sweetheart.

"Hi!, Al."

"H-h-hi, Emy! How... How are you?" Alex managed to ask, somehow. He was, evidently, shocked to see Emily in his house after so many months. She looked beautiful in the yellow dress. He had noticed how she had grown to be a full-bodied woman over the years. He had also noticed scorn in her eyes.

Emily ignored his admiring looks and his "how-are-you's." She had no time for small talk today.

"Al, it's my birthday tomorrow. I have invited most of my friends, and I was wondering if you could make it, too? For old time sakes?"

"Oh! Birthday? Ummm... Yeah, okay." He mumbles.

"It's perfectly okay if you are busy. I was just visiting your neighborhood, so I thought..." Emily deliberated, letting her thoughts hang in the air.

Alex deliberated for a moment. He was not sure why she was there. He felt it was high time to make amends and ignore negative possibilities. He decided to say, "Yes. Hey Emy, I am glad you invited me. I will surely come."

"Okay then, see you tomorrow," Emily hurriedly said, as she turned to go back. Alex and his friend glimpsed her revealing lace panties as her dress moved along with her. Her ass cheeks were so clearly visible, and they were so sexy. Alex had also noticed how her dress top revealed her cleavage. She was surely a turn on.

Emily walked out, smiling satisfactorily. This was easy. She has avoided full contact with Alex throughout the past two months. That, combined with her haughty attitude of today, had left Alex with limited choices.

That night, Emily could hardly sleep. She double-checked the things she had purchased earlier that day. She removed a soft piece of clothing from its packaging and inspected it. She climbed down from the bed, and started to peel off her clothes, one by one. She admired her sexy, naked body in the full-length mirror. She got turned on at the sight of her own sexiness. She looked at the pale blue-colored piece of lingerie in her hand. It is Alex's favorite color. She remembers all his choices, clearly. She tried on her new lingerie and smiled satisfactorily at her reflection in the mirror. Perfect fit! The dress is hiding nothing. Everything was clearly visible. Her rounded tits with light pink nipples were getting erect. Her narrow waist and flat tummy were noticeable. Her sexy, shaven pussy was dripping. Her round, firm ass, as she turned around to admire it, peeked nicely from beneath the dress. Emily felt happy. The dress, as she had presumed, enhanced her nudity and made her more desirable.

Will he still be able to resist her? Will he still be able to say "no" to her? She wished he would. Yeah. She wanted him to say "no." She wanted to seduce him to fuck her. She wanted to dissolve him of his arrogance, punish him for rejecting her. She wanted revenge.

Alexander, too, was not able to sleep. He kept seeing glimpses of Emily's body peeping from the yellow dress. He failed to see how he could be so naïve as to resist such temptation just last year. Emily was sexy even back then, and he could not think of any perfect excuse to justify his behavior last year. He had a steady girlfriend now, but they were not very sexually active. Laura was not half as sexy as Emily.

Sunday, 15th November

Emily was already up and humming, even before the sunrise. D-day was finally here. "Happy birthday... happy birthday," she sang to herself. She was 19 today. She was, officially an adult last year when she turned 18, but not to Alex!

She had already ensured her parents wouldn't skip work because of her birthday. She had told them that she had plans to go out with friends. As soon as she was alone in the house, she started setting up the place. She peeled off all her clothes. Then she pinched her nipples to arouse them. She wanted to be hungry when Alex arrived. So, she tidied up her bed and put on a satiny new bed sheet. She placed incense sticks with amorous fragrances hidden in the corners of her room. She drew the curtains closed. Then, she stocked the fridge with beer, whipped cream, strawberries, and chocolate ice cream. She unpacked the leather whip, collar, and handcuffs. She was ready!

Emily then went for a quick shower and put on the new blue lingerie. She left her hair wet and uncombed. She unlocked the door to her apartment then went into her bed and lay down.

Soon enough, the doorbell rang. She kept lying still. She could hear Alex calling her name. Then she heard the sound of the door opening and footsteps in the living room. She closed her eyes and tried to relax. The door to her room had been kept ajar. Alex keeps calling for her as he nears her room. She senses him coming in, and as the sound of footsteps cease, she knows Alex is standing and staring at her, open mouthed. She held back the desire to smile.

Alex was shell shocked at seeing Emily lying like this on her bed. The room was lit, only by the dim light from the window. Emily looked so vulnerable and beautiful. Her body looked so sensuous in that little blue net and lace she was wearing. He can see all her curves and even her nipples pushing through the thin transparent net. He wanted to hold her and touch her all over. Then, he suddenly got a weird feeling. Is Emily okay? Has someone arrived here before him and hurt her? He got closer and tried to check if Emily was breathing. Yeah, she is breathing, slowly and calmly. She is in a deep, sound sleep. Her chest was heaving up and down as she breathed. He wanted to lick her nipples. He wanted to lick her whole sexy body. She was such a tease, sleeping like this without clothes, and all the doors unlocked. He moved one hand over her heaving tits. She started to stir and opened her eyes.

Emily pretended to be shocked when she saw Alex in her room. "What are you doing to me?" she moaned, as if she were scared. "Did you drug me and are now trying to fuck me, Al?"

Alex panicked at such accusations and asked her to calm down. Emily started shouting instead of calming down.

"Shhh... Em, please! I was not doing anything. I had just arrived when you opened your eyes."

"No! You were trying to fuck me. Where is my birthday dress? I had it on me, before you drugged me to sleep." Emily choked on her words. She was playing the part beautifully.

"Dress? Drugs? No... No, Em! Please, listen to me... Please?" Alex pleaded.

"What, no? I will teach you a lesson, you lecherous bastard. You try and act so innocent, and this is what you do with a lonely girl on her birthday?" Emily was in no mood to let him escape. "I am going to call the police."

He started to shake and falls back, on the bed. Emily didn't waste a moment as she hurriedly chained his hand to the already waiting handcuffs tied to the bedpost. "Al, don't you dare try and escape," she threatened. "You wanted to fuck me? Now, I will show you what a good fuck is all about!"

Alex couldn't help but be turned on by Emily's dominance. She was sexy as hell and though he knew this had to be a game, he couldn't wait to fuck her.

She clamped the leather collar around his neck, switched on the light, and stood in front of him, with her legs spread wide apart and the new leather whip in hand. She looked like a sexy tease. Her long, shapely legs met up into a sexy mound with beautiful lips. Her narrow waist swelled beautifully into shapely, ample tits, and her nipples looked like delicious berries under the blue net. Her slender neck and full lips were no less tempting. She was a sex goddess, a goddess who is, now, in a rage.

Alex was at first confused and shocked, but he knew deep down birthday sex was going to be hot. He played along as if he didn't know how to react. Emily laughed when she noticed him turning pale. She ripped off his shirt to reveal his wide chest. She then pulled down his faded blue jeans. Besides his shock of this sudden seduction, his big cock was hard and animated. She started to whip him on his bare chest, legs, and thighs. He screamed with pain and begged her to stop, though it turned him on more, making his cock even harder. Red welts appeared on his naked body. She threw away the whip and bent down near him.

"Em..." Alex had never played this type of role with his other girlfriends, so he was not able to comprehend what was happening with him. She started to lick the fresh gashes. Her licks burned his skin everyplace he was wounded. She laughed, again.

She moved her tits closer to his mouth. He stayed inert, undecided. "Suck! You bastard, suck my tits. You were ogling at them while I was asleep." He shook his head and turned it to the other side, if she wanted it she'd have to try harder. Emily pulled him by the hair and pushed one nipple into his mouth. He started to lick slowly, mechanically. She closed her eyes and started to moan. He looked at her face. How could such a pretty face act in such a nasty way? Wildcat-like voices coming from Emily slowly turned him on. She got up with a jerk and started to tear away her new dress from the top. Her one breast was completely revealed. Slowly, she tore her dress at several places and it hung on her like net ribbons.

"See what you have done, Al! You despot, you tore my pretty new dress."

"Em? Alex sounded too tired to argue back.

"Ah! I have proof, now, for the police," she winked, wickedly. Her shifting moods, from sensuous to cunning, made him feel dizzy. He was so undecided. He thought he was going to lose his sanity.

She then bent down again and started to lick his cock. Its delicious flavor and hot hardness made her so happy. In wild ecstasy, she scratched him all over his torso and bit him on his thighs. Alex forgot the pain and torture then started to slip into dazed excitement. His dick started to get hard as iron. Emily licked it for a long time, until his pre-cum and her saliva made it slippery. She felt his body relaxing with her licking exercise.

As his dick got hard and ready, Emily climbed onto his hard rod. Facing him, she sat in a kneeling position. She arranged her knees on the bed in such a way that her feet were around the inside of his legs. She moved her upper body a little forward, arching her boobs towards his mouth. Gripping his shoulder with both hands, she pushed against his cock and made it slip in. Slowly and rhythmically, she moved her ass in slow, tight motions. The rhythm accelerated and Emily bounced up and down on him. Her tits jiggled, and he couldn't take his eyes off them. He moved his hands forward and grabbed them. Then, he started to squeeze the nipples. He also started to move his pelvis, to promote her motion. They were moving wildly now. The room was full of erotic sounds and smells. They both came together, after boundless trembling and gasping. She put her head on his chest and moaned, wildly. "Ahhhhhhh... ahhhh, Al.... You are so damn sexy!"

After enjoying her ride, she set Alex free and went out of the room.

"What now?" Alex panicked, again. "Is she really making a call to the police?" He wanted to close his eyes and fall asleep. He knew this was just part of a birthday game.

However, his fears were set to rest, when she came back with a load full of stuff from the fridge. He stared, wide eyed, as she lay down on her tummy and started to pour whipped cream on her lovely ass. She topped it with some ripe strawberries. Her firm, sexy ass looked like a heavenly cake. "It's my birthday, Al! Pamper me... Come on, lick my ass!" she purred.

Alex started to lick away the cream and chew the strawberries. She was amazing. He loved each moment of licking and sucking every drop from her body. Emily was moaning so provocatively, it was tough for him to hold on. He got on again and his dick turned into a wild, hot iron rod. He tried to turn her around and fuck her, but Emily had other plans.

The ice cream had turned soft by now. Emily poured it out all over their bodies, slowly. She spread it, more generously, on his dick and chest, then on her tits and pussy. She smeared her hand with the dark, syrupy liquid that the ice cream had converted into, and rubbed them over his dick. They started licking it off each other. What a lovely birthday treat. They made slow, yummy, messy, crazy love for hours after that. Kneading each other's bodies, licking and biting, with wild urgency. Also, holding, kissing, and caressing. The wild, sumptuous lovemaking went on like a timeless love play. They made love in various positions and came over and over again. Alex was feeling contented and relaxed now. Emily had just played a small trick on him, on her birthday, he mused.

Emily took him to the shower after the long lovemaking and made him clean the mess over her. The wild streak returned to her molten eyes. "Wish me 'Happy Birthday', Al! I am officially an adult, today. You are my first official fuck!" She laughed out loud, as if possessed. She was so happy. Her revenge was complete! Alex's head started to spin as he realizes the implication of those words.

4 THE BOUQUET AT NINE

Preface

The roses never failed to arrive. A beautiful bouquet of one dozen red roses was delivered each night for Sandra Scott exactly at nine. There was never a name on the card accompanying them. Just a line in praise for her body parts, different one each time and signed off as "love." It started with her beautiful black hair and now lingers on her silken thighs. Who is the sender? How does he know so much about her body, as if he has seen her naked, touched her, felt her? Has he? Will he? Let's see....

Sandra's Surprise

David, the caretaker at Central Park Apartments, Downtown Detroit, stared at

Sandra as she walked slowly towards the building. She, though not strikingly beautiful, had a fluid sensuality in her moves. Her white dress glided up her tanned thighs as she floated forward. His stare moved up to her thin waist, which looked too fragile between her rounded ass and those big tits. She was sexy!

David shook his head to clear the thoughts that nighttime duty always brought along. He looked in his register as Sandra moved closer.

"Hello ma'am! You have a bouquet delivered for you," he tried to keep his voice casual as he stared at her cleavage peeping from her dangerously low neckline.

"A bouquet?" Sandra's sleepy eyes opened wide as she looked at David enquiringly.

"Yeah, a bunch of roses, pretty fresh red ones, delivered tonight and the card says it's for you." David smiled as he passed the bunch towards her.

Beautiful, fragrant, dozen red roses exquisitely tied up with ribbon and lace. Lace? Yes, it was lace, lace just like the type they use in...in lingerie! She took the bouquet and climbed the elevator to her floor.

David sighed loudly and moved his hand over the bulge starting to form under his pants. He was horny, like always when on a night shift. He hated to stay away from his new sexy wife. On top of that, the apartments were full of sexy young rich bitches. He can just stare and fantasize. And masturbate? Why not?

While he imagined sucking the huge tits of Sandra and masturbated in his office, Sandra lay in her bedroom staring at the strange bouquet. It was the second in a row. Yesterday, Peter, the watchman, had handed her a similar bouquet. It had a card named to her, "Sandra Scott," with a message neatly typed which read as: "Sandra Scott...this is for your most beautiful tresses...long, black, and sensual with the fragrance of fresh lime and touch of silk. I want them to caress my face as I... Love." The break in message left her imagining many things that would have followed. She had smiled then, thinking it must be someone from the work, teasing her.

She looked at today's bouquet for the card that David mentioned. Ah, here it was, same glossy paper card with same typeface. Her name in bold letters and a note below and signed "love." No name of the sender again. What an expensive way to joke!

The note caught her attention. One line, clear message, that reads, "Sandra Scott...this for your moon-shaped face...fair, beautiful, and satiny soft. I want to inhale the peachy fragrance of your cheeks as I lick them from side to side... Love." Her hand inadvertently went to her cheeks. They were burning hot. She felt suffocated suddenly.

She climbed down the bed and moved towards the bathroom for a shower. She removed her dress and dropped it on the bouquet on the bed. In the shower, she looked at her image in the full-length mirror. The pale skin matched with the ivory-colored bra and panty she was wearing. It was lacy; the same kind in which today's bouquet was wrapped in, the lace style that's her favorite. Is it some of her female friend who sent her the two bouquets?

She shook her head. "...most beautiful tresses...long, black, and sensual...." She closed her eyes, removed her undergarments and turned on the shower. The water was cool and relaxing on her naked body, same for her hair and her cheeks. She felt as if someone wanted to touch them, love them. She shivered. Her hand moved towards the soap case. As she rubbed the soap over her wet body, a peachy fragrance filled the air. She opened her eyes with a start. "I want to inhale the peachy fragrance of your cheeks." Who knows her bathing secrets?

Sandra hurriedly put on her bathing robe and went back to her bedroom. She lived alone in that beautiful and luxurious apartment. She was not new to the city, but after four years of working in New Orleans, she still knew a very few people. Her friend circle is also very limited. She could not think of anyone who could joke this way with her. She decided to wait and watch. Maybe no more bouquets will arrive after tonight. Maybe it's a simple joke and the sender will approach her himself or herself.

But, the roses never failed to arrive. The joke was a long-lived one. A beautiful bouquet was delivered each night exactly at nine. There was never a name on the card accompanying them. Just a line in praise for her body parts, different one each time and signed off as "love."

Day before yesterday, it applauded her soft firm breasts, even mentioning their size and also the color of her nipples! It followed with the desire of the sender to suck them so much so that they stand like ripe red cherries on her fair fleshy mounds. Yesterday, the card made love with her flat stomach and her pierced belly button moving the tongue in its depth till she moaned out loud in delight. And yes, she was really sensitive to touch at around her belly button!

She had tried to get hold of the sender in every way, but each time the bouquet is delivered by a different dispatcher, who never claims a receipt, and handed over to a new person each night at nine. She was having sleepless nights as each card brought about an arousal and also a hidden fear. Is someone trying to seduce her? Or he wants to molest her? Has he really seen her body so up and close, as to know all the fine details? Who is he?

Today's bouquet again had 12 red roses. This time the bouquet was simply left outside her apartment's door. She picked it up and went in her bedroom. Her hands shivered as she took out the card. "Sandra Scott...this for your silken thighs...smooth, firm, and getting wet as I lick them with my hot tongue, moving inwards towards your sexy depths... Love." Sandra's hand unconsciously moved under her skirt on her thighs. Each card on the fragrant bouquet moved one-step forward in making her horny. If the words have so much magic, how much charisma does the sender have? Who is the sender? How does he know so much about her body, as if he has seen her naked, touched her, felt her...? She slept with such thoughts in her mind and dreamed of a stranger making passionate love to her.

Sandra's next bouquet has the sender fingering and licking her pussy, "...my tongue moves in your pale outer lips entering the dark depths of warm silken wetness which pours out in a rivulet as my tongue pokes in and teases the walls of your vagina...the mere thought of your sexy wet triangle makes my junior hard and throbbing." Sandra began fantasizing about having sex with a man she had never met, maybe! She imagined a sensuous young man whose face she could not see. She made love with him in her open-eyed dreams, without knowing anything about him, not even his name.

Someone somewhere fantasized about watching her masturbating in her room with an imaginary man, seeing her body arch in orgasm with her fingers rushing into her.

Sandra was so obsessed now with the bouquet sender that with every man who looks at her admiringly, she thinks, "Is he the one?" She imagined her in bed with many handsome men leering at her. She could think of nothing else but the bouquets and an amorous sender.

Handling the Frustration

One night in a drunken state at a party, Sandra met a handsome man. He kept looking at her all through the night. She imagined him to be the sender and approached him. "Are you looking at my body?" she slurred softly. "Yeah, you have a great one!" He leered at her body hardly concealed in her skimpy strappy dress. He held her arm to stop her from falling. She was way too drunk. "Thank you for the lovely roses!" "Roses?" He couldn't understand but as Sandra moved closer, he held her by her waist. Sandra responded by moving her hands on his back. He took her to the privacy of a side room. Sandra offered no resistance as he removed her clothes and then his own and scattered them around the room. Though Sandra was drunk, she enjoyed the good sex with the mature handsome stranger. She had had enough of imaginative sex! She sizzled as he touched her black tresses, her burning cheeks, her milky breasts with red nipples, her flat tummy, her silken thighs, and her smooth pussy. She orgasmed twice and got bathed in his cum several times all through the night.

After few days, Sandra returned to the same club in hope of meeting the man again. The subsequent bouquets did not mention anything about the lovely sex they had had. Was he the right man? Had she given herself to a total stranger, who hasn't even heard about her before then?

Even after several trips back to the club, she never met that man again. She imagined him telling his friends how he "picked her up" at a party and had sex. He must have thought her to be some nymphomaniac. The sex was exciting, but it was loveless and now Sandra felt silly.

At home in her bed, Sandra kept

thinking about the mess her life has been as of now. She could think nothing but the sex. The bouquets' cards have become more suggestive and sensual in their messages. They have always been such a turn on. Sandra was dying to meet her masked lover but did not want to risk having a casual sexual intimacy with total strangers. She masturbated herself to an orgasm, thinking about her faceless man who sends her roses by the dozen!

One night, she got a card in the bouquet that asked her to come on Saturday night to a secluded spot in her car alone. Sandra got super excited at the thought of meeting "him." It had been three months now that he was pouring expensive love on her. She wanted to return favors now with her exquisite body and elegant sensuality.

She bought a new dress the very next day. It was black and very close fitting. She couldn't wear a bra with it, as it was backless. It had a halter neck that showed the rims of her rounded firm breasts. The dress was so revealing that if she bent or sat down she would exhibit the whole shebang.

The Meeting

Saturday night, Sandra looked very sexy in her new dress and high heels. She thought of even going panty-less, but that would be too bold and desperate statement to make. So she put on black lace panties. She looked in the mirror. Her shapely fair body looked glowing in black satin of the dress. "I hope I meet my dream man today and return with my panties in my handbag!" Sandra winked at herself.

Sandra drove to the lonely spot as mentioned in the card. There were just tall trees there. She was shaking with anticipation. Her hands were between her legs. She was both excited and nervous at the same time. She was thinking, "How can I do this? How can I feel so horny for a man I have never met? My body is already burning with desire! I just do not want to pick up a wrong guy again, and get fucked by him. What if I do not find him appealing?" So many questions popped in her brain like popcorn.

There was no one in sight. Sandra chose to wait. She kept looking all around. Her fingers were moving on her clit over her panties, and that kept her roused. "Maybe everything will work out fine," she thought. "Oh god please let everything go as I have dreamed!"

She got tired of sitting so she parked the car in one corner and got out. The air was bit chilly over her bare skin. She hugged herself with her arms. The more she waited, the more she got confused.

"I don't think I want to do this."

"Maybe he has changed his mind and will not come."

"Maybe it has been all a one long joke."

"Someone somewhere must be laughing at my desperation now."

No positive thoughts came in her mind. Her head starts to spin. She may faint.

"You look so sexy!" a husky male voice right behind her startled her. She spun around to see who it was. Her heart thumped loudly in her chest. There was no one there! Maybe she was hallucinating. She moved around to look behind the row of trees. Her firm ass swayed as she walked in her high heels. Her dress was pulled up and her lacy black panties showed from behind. "Black is my favorite," the same voice again.

Sandra could not understand the joke. Why couldn't she see anyone while the voice is unmistakably coming from somewhere close?

She felt a pair of hands hold her from her waist. Sandra shuddered. The touch was warm and gentle. She moved her hand in the air around her. Her hands brushed something hard, like a human torso. Why can't she see him? She moved her hands over the invisible body standing so close to her. He was a tall slim guy with muscular built. There was not even a single piece of clothing on his body!

The warm skin contact aroused Sandra

and her juices started to flow. She was too exhausted to think clearly. Still, she made a feeble attempt to ask, "Who are you? Why can't I see you?"

A hearty laughter boomed in the air. He brushed his lips on her neck. "I am your desire Sandra. Just feel me." Sandra smiled a weak smile. She was not sure what was happening with her. She wanted to feel him and she could feel herself trembling with desire.

She ran her hands over the invisible body standing inches away from her. The strange invisible lover was a little over six feet tall, and his body was nicely toned and muscled. The guy felt good, tough, and strong. She moved her hands over his eyes, his hairs, his lips, and his nice broad shoulders.

She traced his lips with his fingers and then started to lick them. His skin was burning hot. Sandra knew how madly she wanted him and had wanted him all her life. She sucked in a breath and licked again across his mouth to his neck. Her heart was hammering with exhilaration. As her tongue worked on his upper body, her hands moved on his waist. They moved down to his hips and then to the bulge growing between his legs. He feels hundred percent human. Then why can't she see him?

Sandra trembled a little, indecisive; she

didn't know how to proceed...or should she proceed? But the decision was already made as he had undressed her and pulled her in his arms. Her body started to burn as it came in contact with the hot invisible body. Two unseen arms glided down to her waist while hers went round his neck. She felt her body melting into his. Sandra closed her eyes and stopped thinking. She just wanted to savor the feeling of his hot muscular chest moving against her naked breasts. Sandra tilted her head back and opened her mouth for a kiss. He placed his lips on hers and thrust his tongue in her opened mouth. She let her tongue play with his and moaned softly.

His one hand moved up and cupped her breast. She could feel her nipple harden instantly as he pinched it, making her gasp. His other hand slid to her ass and caressed the cheeks. She removed one of her arms from around his neck and slipped between his legs. The hardness down his leg was bigger and warmer now. She rubbed her hand over it and moaned softly. She pressed closer to him as she squeezed his cock. She was filled with a passionate hunger, and she could hear her heart beating fast. "I want this man to fuck me. I'm going to give myself to this man whom I cannot even see! I'm surely going to do this crazy thing!"

Her thighs started to get wet with her

juices, which were now flowing freely from her pussy. As if on cue, his hand slid between her wetness and he moved a finger over her mound softly but sensuously. He then picked her up and placed her on the hood of her car. He moved between her legs and spread them apart. She put her arms around his neck and let him fuck her mouth with his hot tongue. His big, hard, and warm cock meanwhile rubbed her pussy, making it ooze out more wetness. She spread her legs further by raising her knees and putting her feet on the car's hood. "Fuck me..." her voice was husky with desire and she could hardly whisper. He pushed her gently back in laying position. He pushed his huge cock inside her waiting pussy hole. She arranged her legs around him and guided his manhood into her. He moaned now. His voice was velvety and aroused Sandra all the more. She failed to catch her breath as he started to move inside her. They both moaned as his pace accelerated. Soon, she trembled and let out a long suppressed scream. Her back curved as she climaxed. But he didn't stop; he didn't even slow down and that made her groan with joy as his strokes pulsated her insides. She shouted out loud, "Fuck me! Yes! Yes! Fuck me hard!" as another orgasm peaked in her and left her gasping for breath. But he still fucked her! He kept pounding into her with his still hard hot cock until she could hear him groan and then he squirted once inside her before pulling his dick out. She felt his cock spurting huge amount of warm cum all over her belly and tits like rainfall.

She woke up as dawn was breaking. She was still sprawled on her car's hood, naked. She looked around and found no one. The air was so still and not a sound was audible. She remembered the hot love making of the late evening. Who was the unseen stranger? Has she imagined all that? She climbed down and picked her dress from the ground. As she opened the door, she found a beautiful bouquet on the driver's side seat. The card read, "Sandra Scott...this is for you...the sexiest lady on the planet earth. Thank you for fulfilling my every fantasy of touching you, loving you, making love to you. I want to do it again and again and again...only if you care to return to this place at twilight ... Love."

She had never felt so complete, so ecstatic, so contented.

5 THAT GIRL ON THE STAIRS

Preparing For the Interview

It was raining outside, yet the weather felt stiflingly hot. Darcy looks out of her apartment window with a bored look as she uncertainly fills out the job application form for Mystiques Ltd. She has never heard about this advertising company before. But does she have many choices left? She has been applying all over for a modeling assignment since last month but there have been no results. She signed the form and folded it to put it in the envelope. "I hope I get this one at least," she sighed. She was badly in need of a job, any job!

She'd been at home searching for jobs, willing to do anything for work, even having to fuck strange men for work. Lately, Darcy had fanaticized about having sex with a lot of men at once to make up for the lost time. She'd not had sex in so long; she felt out of tune with her body and couldn't remember what real pleasure felt like other than the use of her vibrator.

Next week, the call from the Mystiques came late in the evening. She had been shortlisted for an interview by the advertising company, the caller informed her. Her mood, grumpy for so many days, perked up a bit at the thought of potential employment, and she started to rummage for a presentable dress for the interview.

Darcy chose a white silk blouse and a short dark blue pencil skirt. As she tried on the dress, she noticed that the skirt now comes a little tight over her ass. Still, the overall effect was beautiful, and she looked like any young model you see in flashy advertisements on the TV. Her soft yet supple breasts filled the thin silk of button-up blouse perfectly and the broad belt of the blue skirt accentuated her slender waist. She wasn't wearing any undergarments as she tried the dress on and her taut dark red nipples peeked out of the thin cloth of her top. She picked up a matching white silk bra to wear with her chosen dress on the interview day. It was trimmed with pretty lace over the bust area.

On the day, Darcy looked into the mirror one last time before picking her matching handbag and locking the front door. She smiled satisfactorily at her attractive image. "Maybe this is the day I get a job or a good fuck," she thought.

The interview was in the evening and in some remote part of the town. She called for a cab and soon was on her way. The busier parts of town faded behind as the cab moved further to new areas at the border of the town. The road here was almost traffic-free; just a random truck or a cargo vehicle crossing them occasionally. Darcy shifted uneasily on the rear seat as she sensed her solitude. She has never been to this part before. The cabby looked harmless and she could not pinpoint any impending danger, but still she could feel droplets of sweat trickling down her thin silk blouse. Her tight skirt was pulled up and revealed a bit of her lace panties as she sat on the edge of the seat. She pulled her skirt down on her legs to cover her modesty. "It is nothing. Just the interview that is making me nervous right now."

Ominous Leanings

The cab dropped her next to the tall building where her interview was scheduled. The building looked deserted She moved hesitantly towards her destination. Her heart thumped loudly in her chest with premonition of some looming peril. She moved towards the elevator. She pressed the button a couple of times but the door refused to budge. She was surprised to notice that there was no staff either at the entrance of the building or near the elevator. It seemed that the elevator was not working. Damn!

Darcy started to climb the stairs. She tried to cheer her nervous mood by thinking of all she would do with her first paycheck. The building had no central cooling system. It was stuffy and hot. She looked up undecidedly. The 17th floor meant a hell lot of stairs! Why the heck the lift had to break down today, of all days? Is fate taking another test of her patience, before she is finally awarded with a glamorous job? She slowly started to climb the stairs, floor by floor.

Darcy was already starting to gasp for breath when she reached the fourth floor. Her high-heeled shoes and tight skirt made the climbing more difficult. She looked around and noticed that she hasn't met a single human being since she had entered the building. She tried to pep up her nervous mood. She tried to think of this as a trekking expedition and kicked her shoes off her feet and held them in her hands. Barefoot, she again started to climb up the floors.

By the sixth floor, Darcy was exhausted. She was sweating profusely and her feet ached like hell. She sat down on a step and pressed her feet with her hands. She reclined her back against the wall. Her skirt moved all the way up her hips. Her blouse was sweaty and was sticking to her tits. She opened a couple of buttons off her white blouse. It was so stuffy in the building. Her skin felt some relief as it gets exposed directly to air. She wiped her handkerchief over legs and arms and moved it over the cleavage protruding out from her white bra. She was thankful that she had no company so far and she could air her sweaty body.

Darcy sat on the stairs for some time. Her limbs refused to move further. But the interview was at 6 p.m.! She had to move on somehow. She made another effort to make her legs work and started to climb the stairs again.

By the 9th floor she was completely drained. Her legs felt like lead and she could hardly move a step without feeling deep pain in her calves. Her body was now hot with all the exertion. Sweat trailed down from her neck in channels, which moved down wetting her bra and running in her skirt to wet her panties before travelling down her legs. She removed her blouse completely as it was getting ruined and stained with sweat. Her bra was almost transparent with wetness of her perspiration. Her red nipples were visible clearly over her fair skin like two ripe cherries over brimming milk cups. She looked down at her sexy body and then up and down the stairs. "No one is around and watching, I will put my top back on at 13th or 14th floor," she mused.

Darcy again sat down on the stairs. She needed water. Her head was whirling with the exertion and heat. She rested her head on the wall and closed her eyes bleary with sweat. Moving forward even an inch seemed impossible to her. Soon Darcy dozed off on the stairs.

After some while, Darcy hears a sound on the stairs. She woke up with a start. She was unable to place her whereabouts for few minutes before she remembered the interview. The stairs were darker than when she was climbing them. It seemed she had slept for a good long time. She again heard that sound, like some shuffling footsteps. She noticed her almost naked body and pulled her blouse over her chest to cover her bulging tits.

Things Take A Turn

"No use wrapping up now lady, I've seen the whole package." The voice came from just beyond the turn four steps ahead of her. She looked in the direction of the voice. A shabby middle-aged man walked down from the stairs. He was dressed in working overalls, which were stained with grease and paint. He was somewhat handsome, you could tell he had a long day's work, but with a good shower and cleaned up, he's not bad on the eyes at all.

This was not the ideal situation, she did have an interview, at the sight of this strange man, her state of dress or lack there off, and she was starting to feel turned on. She needed to play her cards right, she didn't want this eye to think she was too easy. She was going to play out her fantasy of sex with a stranger right now.

"Who are you and what do you want?" Darcy yelled as if to sound panicked. Her heart started to thump in her chest but she tried to keep the any type of seduction away from her voice.

"I am Martin and what I want depends on what you have got!" he grinned a wicked smile at her. His was a tall and hefty man. His grin was wicked and that turned her on even more, a strange man wanting to have his way with her. He looked at her partly covered chest and sneered, "From what I've seen you've got enough."

Darcy tried to look shocked. She had never imagined such a situation ever in life. The worst possible for today was a job rejection. But the possibility of a fantasy filled for a good fuck finally, she shivered.

"Stay away," she retorted, "I have people waiting for me upstairs and they may come down if I do not reach them on time."

Martin laughed. "I won't mind them people," he said, "If you want, I can call them down for you." The comment startled Darcy and she looked at him questioningly.

He looked up the stairs and whistled. Three more men, dressed in similar dirty overalls peeped down. Darcy shivered visibly this time. To make things worse for her, Martin beckoned the guys downstairs with one hand and with his other hand he lecherously cupped his crotch.

Darcy pulled the shirt over herself, hiding her nearly naked chest but one of the men moved towards her and snatched it from her hand. This was going to be better than she first thought. Not only could she have one stranger but a group of men fuck her. She'd have to step up her act. Perhaps if she cried and begged they would surely take advantage as in her fantasy.

"Please...let me go. Please?" Darcy begged. Her voice cracked now and tears started to stream down her pretty face.

"Hey, hey do not cry my pretty maid. We will make you happy. We noticed you were trying to cool your hot body yourself. I hope you will appreciate our help and love to have some nice hard cock, won't you?" Martin leered. They all looked at her tits and her legs and the small piece of blue cloth covering her panties. She looked deliciously tempting.

Martin started to move closer to Darcy. Darcy tried to look panicked. She hasn't had sex in the past year since she broke up with her boyfriend. She had been having so many cock fantasies and sleeping with men. The thought of four huge men forcing themselves inside her didn't scare her at all, in fact it made her wet. Her pussy is so tight right now; she had just hoped her cunt would be able to take the pressure from all the cocks. She already started shiver at the thought of the anticipated intrusions.

Martin started to pull her skirt off from her waist. She looked at the other three men as they just stood there grinning. Martin seemed to be their leader. Darcy tried to move back from his hold, but there was no space backwards. She wanted a more comfortable spot and to make the men think she was scared. She got up and started to run upstairs. Martin gripped her skirt tight and it ripped apart from her body.

Darcy ran in her panties and bra soaked with sweat as fast as her limbs could let her. The men looked up at her nearly naked body. "I'm not sure about you guys," Martin said, "But I know I'd love to relish some of that sexy body." He followed Darcy, and in few laps grabbed her leg and pulled her down. Darcy fell down and sprawled in midst of four ravenous men. Their eyes were fixed on the skimpy panties covering her modesty. The tallest of them pulled it off her body in a single movement. "Great Job Smith, she got the neatest meat pie I ever laid my eyes on," said Martin as he pointed and gawked at the neatly trimmed triangle at the meeting of her thighs.

Darcy tried to sit up but Smith pushed her roughly back onto the stairs. "Now, now, young lady, don't be childish! You know you cannot fight us so do not waste your energies in running about. I am sure you would love some nice big cock."

Darcy was about to say something, when Martin yanked the zip of his work trousers down and revealed his long thick cock. For a moment, Darcy's fake panic turned into awe. She had never tasted something so huge. But she won't let them how sex-starved she had been. She didn't want the strange men to know how much she was going to enjoy sex with all of them.

"Hey, Mike, Smith, Josh I am going in first, anyone mind?" Martin boomed out loud. He looked mad with desire. Darcy looked around and saw all other three men he had addressed shook their head as they kept staring at her body. They had already unzipped their trousers and begun rubbing their cocks. "God! They all have such big cocks," gasped Darcy.

She shook her head to ward off such feelings of want in her, if they saw she wanted it, they may not fuck her as good as she wanted. She knew they were going to gangbang her and she was going to enjoy every minute. It was going to be quite easy to cooperate with their demands she thought. Little do they know, they were part of her own little sexual fantasy. But her body refused to listen to her. She could feel her tits enlarging and nipples going erect. Her hand moved to her tits as she again tried to get up. She crawled a few stairs upwards. Martin held her waist and pulled her closer. He picked her up and took her up the stairs.

"You want to love me up there? Come, I will take you sweetiem" his hot breath burned her neck. He placed her on the landing of 10th floor and removed her bra. He tossed Darcy's bra down the stairs. "I think now it is the perfect view," he said as he ogled down at Darcy's nude body. Her rosy pink nipples stood out from her fleshy mounds. Darcy placed a hand over her nipples to hide them.

"Please," she continued with her fake fear, "let me go." Her heart was beating so loud now and she feared Martin could hear it. She could feel her thighs go wet with her juices in anticipation of the pleasure she was going to get from these four studs.

"Let you go?" Martin asked, "Well we've got a lot of fun to give to you before we can let that happen." He looked down at his three workmates. "What do you think guys, should we help the lady out?" In response to his query, the three men climbed up the stairs to the landing where Darcy was lying. They were still rubbing their cocks, which have turned inflated now. Darcy was encircled by for muscular men, each with their cock in their hand.

She looked around her with eyes wide open and waited for the attack. She should panic and scream about, struggle to appear as though she wanted to get away from them, but it was the exact opposite. She wanted to yell for them to fuck her now! She stayed still looking at them and thinking that this is going to be an evening to remember.

The men began stripping off. Now Darcy was surrounded by four unclothed men, each with a taut enlarged cock. "Now my sweet sexy lady," Martin asked her, "Which one of us you want first? It really doesn't matter anyways as you're going to get us all sooner or later."

Darcy didn't have time to reply, as Martin had already stepped forward. "I'll pump her tight holes first of all, if you don't mind guys." The three men move bit backwards giving Martin all the space to relish the sexy bait.

"Come on Marty! Fuck the lady hard," Josh replied, "Get her all lubed up for our use later."

Darcy clinched her legs together, keeping up the charade of struggle.

"Oh, she's acting hard to get friends!" Martin said. "Josh, Mike, hold the girl's legs buddies as I show her what a big hard cock feels like." The men did as Martin commanded and walked over to either side of Darcy's legs and gripped an ankle each and forcefully yanked her legs apart, exposing her pussy for the penetration of Martin's cock.

Martin climbed over Darcy and stood between her legs. He then knelt on the stairs and rubbed his swelling cock through her pussy lips. As Martin touched the tip of his huge cock over Darcy's pussy, he screamed with joy. "Guys! She is all wet already; the horny bitch is looking forward to all the fun."

"She's got a really sexy cunt buddies" said Josh as he peeped in between her legs. "Yeah and it is so snug," Martin grinned. He grabbed her boobs as he pushed his cock in and out of her pussy hole.

"Hurry up Marty, dig her fast man, there are three more cocks here that want to pump that tight hole," Mike shouted as he looked at his wristwatch. Martin, understanding his signal, wasted no more time and hurriedly pumped Darcy's pussy. Darcy felt his balls bumping her pussy lips as he thrust his hard cock in and out. She tried made an effort not to respond, but she, being the woman she was, let out a long low moan as the cock quickly moved in her hole.

This was it. She was finally getting her fantasy loved the feeling all her pussy getting filled by these strange men. The pleasure and fullness of getting fucked after going so long without sex couldn't be described.

"Already told you, she's enjoying it," Martin said as he shoved his full size into her. "Hey girly, you are loving it, aren't you?" he said as he thumped deeper into Darcy's pussy. "Your wet tight cunt loves it, isn't it?" Martin repeated his query again and again. Darcy didn't mean to answer him but as Martin whacked into her hard and asked again, "Isn't it?" She gasped out loud and said in a breathless voice, "Yes."

That was what they all wanted to hear. Martin began banging his cock into her faster and harder now. Mike, Josh and Smith meanwhile rubbed their dicks in expectancy of upcoming erotic fun.

After a while, Darcy felt Martin's whole

body has become rigid. "Oh! Ohhh fuck! I'm cumming...I'm cumming!" he gasped and Darcy felt his cock shudder inside her. "Ohhhhhh Godddddd," David boomed, "Here it fucking comes. Yeahhhh!"

The flood of cum erupted inside Darcy as Martin discharged his cum inside her pussy. He moaned loudly with each release. He took about another two minutes before Darcy felt his cock shriveling inside her. Finally, he pulled it out of her hole and made way for Mike.

Mike nearly pushed Martin aside as he took his place between Darcy's legs and slid his long cock into her pussy hole in one rapid move. Darcy's pussy offered no opposition, as it was full of Martin's cum. Mike easily pounded away at her, thumping the full length of his cock into her wet pussy again and again. "Oh damn, she is so fucking sexy. This is gonna be my best fuck in a long time!" It was not long before Darcy felt his cock blowup within her.

Darcy noticed that two men have already cum inside her and she has yet to achieve an orgasm. Her pussy was full of double cum-loads, which felt as if she had herself cum. She relaxed her body anticipating being filled by the rest of them men awaiting their turn. No need to keep up the facade as if she wanted to escape, the ordeal she was getting the satisfaction of four cocks. Now she wanted to cum.

After Mike finished, who didn't take long, Josh and Smith were ready to take their turns. Soon Darcy's pussy was oozing cum of four guys and even she was able to cum a couple of times as she started to enjoy the action.

Later the four naked men stood over her nude wet body with their drooping cocks dangling between their legs. Darcy looked around undecidedly. Then she thought of an idea and smiled. She reached out and took Josh's and Smith's cock in each of her hands. "Hey the lady wants more," Martin said happily. "Then she would have to help us getting hard for her this time." Darcy knew precisely what he intended and extended her neck towards his cock. Martin smiled down at her.

She readily put his cock inside her warm mouth and started to suck him greedily. Meanwhile she rubbed two cocks in her hands. Mike moved behind Darcy and started to rub her tits from behind. He pushed her forward towards Martin's cock and inserted his cock in her asshole. Darcy screamed out loud. She is handling four cocks in one go now.

"Wow she is such a treat," Mike said and they all laughed. All the cocks soon recovered their hardness. "Round two,"

Josh shrieked.

They again took turn of getting between her legs and pumping her pussy and asshole with their hard cocks. This time they were not so swift in cumming, and they gave Darcy the chance to orgasm every time the men took their subsequent chance at her.

As Darcy lay on the stairs, later, with cum overflowing from her pussy, she had a smile of satisfaction on her face and not the turmoil of being violated or a victim. It's what she wanted.

She watched the men dress up and move down the stairs. She closed her eyes and counted the fucks and sucks she had that evening. Not bad for an evening, she smiled.

Interview completely forgotten. "Well, I guess I didn't get that job, but I sure did get my fantasy."

6 WITHOUT YOU

Left Alone

I smiled absently, not really listening to Elizabeth as she talked excitedly about her trip on way to the airport. She is never disturbed or at unease. At least, I have never seen her agitated over anything over the past ten months we have been together. Less than an hour ago, she was in my arms...sizzling and passionate. Now, she is going away to London. Okay, it is just for three days, but still she will be away!

I guess I was sulking like a teenager. I had been since morning. It was all wrong. I was the one who encouraged her to go on this trip. I never thought it would be a big deal, this short separation between Liz and me. She had been looking forward to this international fashion show, and I realized how important it was for her to travel to London just now. It may prove to be a great career boost for my young aspiring fashion model girlfriend. But then, I had all the plans to accompany her. I never knew then that these surgical emergencies would crop at the hospital and I would be stuck up here in New York.

"Dr. Michael White, you are far away already?" Liz waved a hand in front of my face. "Eh? No, I was just thinking about the hospital."

"Hospital? Some hot nurse joined?"

I have never found Liz serious or sad or even a teeny-weeny ruffled. And that's why I loved her this much. I mean liked her....

It is a beautiful bond that we two share. It has not even been a full year since I met Elizabeth at a social gathering. My liking for this young budding fashion model was instant. The moment she entered the party hall, her great body, her shining blue eyes, and her copper hair lured me in her enticing charisma. But it is not just her hourglass figure, but her effervescence and cheery outlook that made us gel. Though she is almost half my age, her response to my overtures was also no less quick. Most women tell me I have a masculine appeal which most females fall for.

Within a week of our first night together, Liz had moved into my apartment, as it was big and convenient. There has never been any commitment, no strings attached, just a union of convenience. It was a convenience of a happy and satisfying co-existence. She had been a bubbly and cheerful company. I have always loved to experiment in bed, and Liz was always more than eager to cooperate.

She kissed me on my mouth as she said her byes, flashing her best smile that she knows will cheer me up.

"Come on, it's only three days Mike!"

"Liz, that's four nights for god sake!"

I had almost shouted out. She giggled and told me not to act like a 40-year-old teenager. I pulled her closer and hugged her tight. She patted my cheek lovingly and started to walk towards the check-in.

I looked admiringly at her sensuous gait. She had a great body. Her tight ass swayed in her cotton dress. How I longed to grab her and take her back home. I pulled away my gaze with much effort.

It was way past midnight when I reached home. Everything seemed so empty without Liz. I undressed slowly and laid down on the king-sized bed, alone after so many nights. Sleep was far away from my eyes. Nothing constructive to do, I started to browse through my collection of pictures on my cell, mostly of me and Liz, reliving each moment together. The sweet memories made me yearn for her. I could almost imagine Liz in the bed with me, warm, naked and welcoming. My hand moved on its own will over the bulge that started to form in my boxers.

"Liz! When will you come back?"

The wait had just started, but it was already becoming unbearable for me. Is she missing me too? Or is she too excited about her trip to even think about me? I picked up my cell phone and dialed her number, cancelling the call immediately afterwards as I realized she must be in her flight.

Just My Imagination

Somehow, I fell asleep while watching a movie on the television and had been asleep for a while when I woke up to a loud noise outside. It was three in the morning, and I saw a couple having sex on the TV screen in some late-night movie. The lady was being fucked hard by her partner, and her breasts jiggled as he shook her. I missed Liz terribly. I recalled how delightful it was to make love to her. Liz loved staying topless when at home, and her milky white breasts were always inviting. I wanted her to suck my cock right now and make it big enough to penetrate her deep and nice. The woman in the TV mounted her beau and started to ride him. My attention again went to her lovely bouncing breasts. Her moans made my breath warm and my heartbeat fast. I pushed my hand in my boxers and rubbed my growing junior. Slowly, it grew big enough that it couldn't be held caged in the tight shorts. I pulled down my boxers and concentrated on the sexy tits of the naked lady on TV. I heard myself moan as I imagined tweaking her pink nipples. "How pleasing it would feel to have my cock buried deep inside her," I thought as I closed my eyes and rubbed my cock fast attuned to the sounds of the TV couple moaning and sighing. I could feel myself getting close to orgasm, so I moved my hand faster. I was breathless and panting. With each thrust of my hard dick inside my hand, my groaning got louder. I climaxed with a sharp seizure, and my cock shot out cum all over my legs and stomach. My heart still raced fast as I stretched out on my bed with her tits on my mind and a somewhat satisfactory smile on my lips.

Next day, I kept myself busy with work. But at night, the pangs of separation again gripped me. Imagining her and lying awake till small hours, naked and playing with my own hands, was not going to do much good. So this time, I called up Liz.

Her soft sensuous voice on the other end of the line triggered an instant arousal.

"I am missing you baby!"

"I am missing you too, hon."

She told me she was back in her hotel room after the day's work and just had a bath. Liz fresh and fragrant from her bath must be looking awesomely tempting in her nightgown. I couldn't believe how soon I turned on just from the sound of her husky   voice.

"Liz, I am missing your sexy body too."

I could envision her smiling seductively on the other side of the line. I closed my eyes and pictured myself lying between her legs.

"Liz I want to make love to you," I whispered.

"Then do it," she whispered back, "do it with your words, fuck me over the phone. I am also so hungry for you Mike! Tell me all the ways you will touch my body and let me feel the familiar rousing deep within my body. Make me lose myself to carnal pleasures Mike. Fuck me please, fuck me over the phone."

My body quivered with her reply.

"Liz! Get naked then honey just the way I am now. Imagine I am watching you as you strip off your clothes one by one. Get rid of them," I whispered to her.

"They are on the floor Mike. I am looking at you temptingly before unhooking my pink ribbon and lace bra. It has joined the clothes pile on the floor!"

Liz replied back in her sensuous voice.

"I am pulling down my tiny lacy dark pink panties. I am naked now... waiting... come on."

"I can imagine your big firm breasts Liz! Your pink nipples are so perked up that I want to put them in my mouth. Now, move back and let me see your shaven young pussy."

Liz could hear me gasp. She must have smiled her sparkling smile as I asked her to turn around and show me her firm round ass.

"Ah Liz! How I love to play with your tender breasts... and how you squirm on the bed as I touch them, wrinkling the bedspread as you move your ass."

She moaned softly over the phone. I closed my eyes again and pictured my hands on her.

"Liz imagine my hands rounded up to your perked-up nipples. I will make them hard by rolling them between my fingers. I will massage your large tits and lick their shiny surface."

"Mike... my nipples are erect and waiting for your bites. Cover my body in tingles as you move your hand on every inch of me. I want to cum for you so badly!"

"Liz, I run my finger over your cute swollen clit and see your body tremble. I will make light circles around the clit, making sure to tease your outer lips with my middle finger."

She moaned again, hearing my voice loaded with lust over the phone.

"I quicken the pace with my fingers, changing between rubbing your clit Liz and slowly sliding my middle finger into your cunt and squeezing against it." Her breathing began to quicken over the phone and even my moans came more frequently, nearly with each breath. I heard a familiar buzzing sound from my earpiece.

"Liz, is that what I am thinking it is?"

I can imagine her smiling softly as she replied.

"Yeah, Mike I packed it with your memories, my pink vibrator from the bedside table."

"Tell me what you are doing"

I wanted to hear her sexy voice as I held my hard hot cock in my hand and imagined her playing with it.

"I am holding the vibe with one hand, and it is on as you are listening to its soft buzz. I am tracing it around my breasts, moving over my nipples. I am so horny Mike! My hips are writhing against the bed. My pussy is dripping honey, and I am aching for your touch. But I have this vibe instead, and I am now moving it gently over my shaven pussy."

Liz detailed her actions so perfectly that I could almost see her next to me on my bed.

Her voice purred through my mind as she told me that she had slipped the vibrator between her lips.

"I can feel it brush my puffy clit. Ahhhhhh..." she moaned loudly. "With my other free hand, I am grabbing my breast. Now, the vibrator slide up and down the length of my lips. It is delighting my clit and exciting my opening."

"What was that?" I asked her as she moaned out loud again.

"I have slipped the vibrator into my pussy Mike," she could barely speak and continued with several moans... "I have clasped the vibrator firmly with my pussy, and I am pushing it further in. Ahhh.... It is in, almost the entire length. Now, slowly, I began to pull it back out, the vibration still stimulating my hard clit. Back in went the vibrator. I began to quicken the pace, in and out, my free hand massaging my breast and tweaking my nipples."

Now, her moans came almost with each breath. My head filled with thoughts of her naked body, her flat tummy, and her big tits and round ass. I imagined her making love to the pink vibrator getting breathless and horny.

"Mike, think of what I could be doing to you and slowly move your hand between your legs and touch the tip of your penis just where you want my tongue to be. Oh wouldn't it be good to be licked just there by my impatient tongue? Come on, let your finger rub your hard dick gently but quickly and you feel the pre-cum start oozing out."

Liz never sounded so damn sexy!

I was so shaky and horny by now as I obeyed her soft commands and imagined her shift her legs wider and moves her vibrator in her wild pussy. Her moans and gasping breaths made me all the more wild.

"Mike, feel my pussy opening up and the vibe getting so wet. Aahhhhhh honey, I am feeling so hot! Tell me what you are doing with my little love there."

I stroked my huge dick with my hands and imagined her legs open up wide and her slimy pussy dripping with juices. "Oh Liz, I want you to suck me," I moaned loudly. "You don't know how much I want you just now Liz!" I almost begged to her.

Her sexy voice gripped me in sexy fervor, and I started to feel pressure build up in my cock. Her sexy little act in the hotel room so many miles away made my cock so buzzing and hot and wild that within minutes I could feel myself shake as orgasm rushes out from deep inside.

"Mmmmmm.....aahhhhhh...Oh yes!"

I smacked my lips as I imagined Liz licking off my hot cum from my thighs. I rubbed my cock to drip off the last drops of cum and then stood up a little shaky. I took a paper towel and cleaned my cock.

"Mike, heat is radiating from between my legs."

Liz was still so horny on the other end. "Come lick my pussy!" she was again inviting me to a hard on. My cock had gone a bit limp by then, but it wouldn't mind more action. I grabbed my cock and start to rub it again with fresh urgency. "Mmmmmmm.... Aahhhhhhh.... I love you Mike," her husky voice sounded so good that my manhood got erect instantaneously to salute her sexuality.

"Ahh. Hmmmm. Oh, yes..." moans escaped from her lips. And then louder, "Oh, god, yes....let it happen. Ahhhh!" she screamed.

I rubbed my fat hard cock as I fantasized her naked body squirming on the bed lustily. Her hips must be wildly thrashing about as the vibrator rushes up and down along her glistening opening. Her breasts must be nodding up and down and her large, lovely pink nipples invited him. She was now groaning with desire and told him that the vibe is on max speed.

"Come fuck me harder now....Mike..." Liz cried. She was going nuts with the working of vibrator. "Aaahhhhhhh... aahhhhhh... aaahhh... delight my clit, tease my pussy...aaahhhhh...." It was getting too much for me now. I could hardly breathe. I gripped my cock slippery with precum, harder. Pleasure shoots up and down the length of my cock. Now, we both are making sensual sounds as we worked on our bodies.

Liz must have squeezed her pussy tightly around the vibrator as I could hear her repeated shouts "Yes... yess.... yessss...!" We could feel our climax build up. Soon my body begins to tense. I held my breath and closed my eyes tight as the climax mounted.

She moaned my name again and again, as she pushed her vibrator in and out of her pussy. Her moans made me quiver. I closed my eyes and thought of her beautiful face as my cum surged out in heavy rush. The ejaculate gushed out in such spurts like I had never cum before!

The sound of vibrator ceased and Liz let out a long sigh. Her voice sounded still breathless and husky as she breathed, "I love you Mike."

"You liked that?" I was grinning as I asked her. "Ohhh yeahh... yeah, I loved it Mike," she sounded happy too.

I looked at the bedside clock, and it was 3 a.m. I asked her to sleep before her next modelling schedule lest she had puffy eyes.

I lay down too with a smile on my face

as I thought of the vivid and delightful memory we have gifted each other today. The whole thing was simply amazing. I felt so content without even actually doing the act.

7 THE TRIPLE TROUBLE

Jacob looked at his watch time and time again. He was sure he had an appointment with Mandy at three in the afternoon; he had confirmed it this morning. With nothing else to do, he had arrived early and there were still a few minutes until his appointment. The bar had a deserted look at this time of the afternoon. "Good!" thought Jacob. He liked to keep his affairs discreet, especially the affairs that involved paid pleasures.

Tired of waiting, he banged his third empty beer bottle on the table and went out. He stood at the doorway. With a bored expression, he looked towards the crossroads and suddenly he had a big surprise. He saw three pretty girls coming from different directions, and they all looked stunningly tempting. They all seemed to be approaching the bar. He stared really hard and scratched his head. He looked confused, but for a split second only. How could he be so silly to invite all three of them at the same time? Something went wrong surely, and he had messed up, really messed up big time, and now only he could save his own skin. His thoughts began to run haywire.

All three ladies were his rich young clients, not to mention "hot and sexy" too. Would he be able to resist even one of them? What, with the money they may shower on him after being satisfied and all the fun they may have? He decided he has to either choose one or have all three together. But could he take all three of them together? Would his cock be able to take up that much load? He knew them from a past couple of experiences and they were horny bitches. He made some mental calculations, and the various possibilities made him shiver with excitement. He was going to have a triple trouble today, and he was going to come out victorious and rich.

Girls often told him that his cock shoots an incredible amount of cum. When he is so hard and worked up and finally cums, it's usually a huge load. It was enough to feed the hungry assholes and mouths and shower on the perky tits and flat tummies, still dripping in abundance on the floor. Not many lovers could handle all his man's juice on their own. Maybe it could be divided between the three horny women, who looked like they may pounce on him in few minutes. He let out a happy sigh as he decided to earn thrice in one go.

As the women reached him, he was already initiating his plan of action. He greeted them and seated them on a low couch in a corner of the bar. He pretended as if he deliberately mixed up their timings to make it a fun-filled foursome experience. A little hesitant at first, Jacob was surprised and satisfied that none of them really objected to the idea.

He introduced them to each other, starting with 23-year-old Mandy, with her long body and red hair. She was a student at a local university and came from a rich family. The other two girls stared at her slim athletic body and her small breasts. Her nipples looked large as they stuck out of her thin cotton top. Then there was Cathy, a 28-year-old married woman. Her rich husband was always away on business, leaving the horny wife searching for paid love. She was a brunette with a hot body and large breasts. His third date for the day was the most beautiful 18-year-old schoolgirl he had ever met, Hazel. She was a young blonde with a thin, short, and shapely figure. They had met at a party and a drunken Hazel had practically pseudo-raped him that night. He had enjoyed sex with her so much that he let their first session go for free.

He took all three women to the big room above the bar. His friend, the bar-owner, had let him use his rooms free of cost for his sexual work in return for some shared sexual fun.

He mixed drinks for all of them. After passing out drinks to the ladies, he went in the shower for a quick clean. As he emerged out of the bathroom five minutes later, he sensed the three women more comfortable with each other, giggling and chatting in whispers. It seemed as if they had ganged up against him... or was it in his favor?

"What's up ladies?" he asked.

They giggled together again. Hazel walked up to him and asked him to put on his jeans. Then all three asked him to follow them.

"No shirts!" Cathy yelled.

The three girls removed their shirts and left them behind. Clad in bras or bikini tops and shorts, they pulled Jacob towards Cathy's car that was waiting outside. Hazel took charge of the steering wheel as the other two sandwiched Jacob between them in the rear of the convertible.

Mandy and Cathy started to caress his

naked torso. Their hands moved all over his chest and back, and they started to kiss him on his cheeks and neck. Jacob pulled them both closer and moved his hands to their tits.

"I'd love to see the fun in the backseat," said Hazel as she adjusted the rear view mirror towards the backseat. She looked at them and giggled. Cathy was kissing Jacob wildly while he fondled Mandy's tits. They didn't notice where Hazel was taking them.

Hazel stopped the car near an isolated spot on the beach and got out. The others joined her on the sunny beach. This part of the beach was away from the crowded city and no one was around. All three girls lined up in front of Jacob and started to remove their shorts. They were in bras and panties now and looked seductive and mouthwatering. Before Jacob could plan a move, three pairs of hands were all over him. The hands moved not only on his naked chest and back, but also tried to enter his jeans.

Cathy asked Jacob in her deep sexy voice for him to drop his pants. He shivered with excitement as he removed his jeans.

"The boxers too..." whispered Mandy. He removed his boxer shorts and his excited dick shot up, ready to put on a show for the women around him. His dick began to stiffen quickly under their steady gaze. They yelled with thrill and giggled and gently touched it like excited children upon seeing a new toy. Hazel dropped to her knees and reached out and took his member in her soft hands. She looked up at his face and began gently stroking him.

Mandy and Cathy dropped their bras to the ground and even pulled Hazel's bikini top from her back. While Mandy rubbed her small tits with protruded nipples on his back kissing him all over, Cathy put one breast in his mouth. Jacob grabbed one of Hazel's jiggling tits in his hand. Hazel played with his big cock and he got very excited. He needed to shoot a load of cum.

Cathy leaned over and whispered softly in his ear, "Want me to suck you off? I think the junior there needs it."

"Oh yes, please suck my cock!" Jacob exclaimed impatiently.

Cathy moved Hazel back and sat down on the sand and pulled the erect cock to her warm mouth and let it slip in. Hazel moved back and pulled her panties down. Jacob noticed she was dripping wet. Now Mandy moved in front and let him suck on her boobs. They grew heavy and taut as he sucked and bit them.

Cathy caressed the large head of his big cock with her soft lips and smooth tongue. Jacob groaned as she skillfully used her tongue and lips on his ever-growing member. Almost without warning, his sac constricted and sent a hot flood of cum into her mouth. The hungry cocksucker, Cathy, drank down every drop, not allowing even a single droplet to slip away from greedy mouth.

Cathy then quickly stood up and immediately removed her panties, which were soaking wet by now. Her supple body with ample and full breasts gleamed in the bright sunlight. She was Jacob's favorite – a sexy insatiable horny bitch! She had a body that was made to be used by strong men. Her large tits jiggled as she moved, her erect nipples imploring to be sucked by a hungry mouth. He grabbed her by her tits and pulled her closer. Mandy bent down to suck on his cock.

Hazel sat on a huge boulder facing Jacob and started to rub her hand over her dripping shaven pussy. She moaned seductively as she watched them playing with each other's bodies. She spread her legs wide and pushed a couple of fingers in her tight love hole. Jacob gasped at the lovely sight. She was such a tease.

The three women played with his cock a long time, taking turns sucking and licking it.

Jacob was surrounded by overpowering feminine allure, shapely tits, and taut full asses and amazingly smooth shaven cunts. He was turned on like never before. He felt like digging his cock in all the holes available to him just then.

Hazel moved closer to Jacob, arched her back, and jutted her young chest towards him. He moved his mouth from the dark nipples of Cathy to take Hazel's cherry-sized nipples. Jacob practically dove at them, sending them both tumbling back on the warm sand. He was wild now.

As he chewed on the fleshy tits of Hazel, he stroked his hard-on against her soft wet pussy. Cathy and Mandy positioned themselves near the pair and started some hot lesbian play. They sucked and licked at each other's tits and pussies, making them more wet and ready.

Hazel was panting hard and her cunt was leaking like a water faucet. Jacob could sense that she was turned on to the max and in dire need of a good hard fucking. He used his leg to spread her legs wide apart. His cock was now hard as steel. Teasing her, he dripped his tongue inside her cunt hole. The hungry tongue probed the wet crack on her fleshy mound.

"Ohhhhh.....goddd....aaahhhhh...." Hazel moaned loudly. His tongue moved over her responsive lips and moved in and out of her pussy. Cathy copied him and stuck her tongue in Mandy's love hole placing her own cunt on Mandy's mouth so she could return the favor. They all moaned in various tones. A kind of sexual orgy was taking place in broad daylight on an open beach. Loads of cunt juice spilled over the sandy seashore.

Before Hazel had a chance to catch her breath, Jacob got to his knees and put his enlarged rod on her waiting pie. In an instant and in one hard shove, he buried his dick deep inside her wet and hot fuck hole. She screamed out loud as her tight pussy was filled with his enormous cock. Jacob pounded furiously and Hazel curled her legs around his back. Her young soft tits jiggled with every thrust. Jacob came for a second time released his cum all over Hazel's legs and stomach.

As he released her for a clean up, Mandy grabbed his legs and started to clean his cock with her tongue. Jacob felt as if he was in a heaven full of sexy angels. Mandy locked him in her grip, sucking hungrily at his cock that was dripping with cum. She almost seemed to beg him like a whore to fuck her hard. Jacob wasn't sure he would get another hard-on this soon, but with nude Mandy between his legs and two nude girls moving about, his cock was up and ready in only moments.

He smiled at how these girls who looked sophisticated and uptight from outside were all little bitches that could even beg in need of sexual respite and would say or do anything to achieve it.

Soon he was doing Mandy doggy style and she was moaning so loud with excitement and pleasure. Her thin body was folded between his legs, and his big cock was moving in her tight hole with varying rhythms. Just before he was about to cum for the third time, he pulled her face up to admire the helpless girl. For the third time in less than an hour, he emptied his cum over the ass of a beautiful young girl.

He loved every second of the paid sexual assignment he had on his hands that day. It was going to be a long, memorable afternoon for him. As Mandy regained her breath, they both got up and patted off the sand from their asses. He stared at the other two girls who had moved in the seawater and were cleaning themselves, helping each other.

He and Mandy joined Hazel and Cathy, who were frolicking in the sea like two naked kids. They played with the water, laughed and giggled in pure ecstasy. After cleaning themselves, they came out fresh from the sea. Their naked bodies glistened in the sunlight. They lied down together on the beach, content.

In some time as Jacob almost dozed off, he felt a feeling of lust and desire washing over the girls again. They stirred their naked bodies lazily on the sand, and their hands started to move on his legs, chest, and neck. He sighed happily at the thought of another round of sex games with all the three players. With closed eyes and just following his sense of smell, he started eating the pussy closest to him. Hard nipples and soft tits brushed over his naked chest. The lucky cock was pretty soon rock hard and his red end throbbed with energy. Someone took his cock in their mouth and groaned seductively. Jacob smiled, enjoying each sensation with closed eyes. He just wanted to grab, feel, and eat the three beauties that he had mistaken at the bar as triple-trouble.

In no time they were again groaning with pleasure, and the sand again started to smell of pheromones and love juices.

With three hot beauties all over him, Jacob thought he was one lucky bastard enjoying a triple sundae!

8 LOVE OF A SHADOW

Prologue

I think back to the experience and I am still not sure whether it was real or simply a dream. I do know however, that it was the most sexually erotic experience of my entire life, and I will never forget it. Even though it happened just a few months ago, it is fresh in my mind as if it just happened yesterday.

The Shadow Woman

It was a chilly autumn night outside, so I went around my house and closed and locked all of the windows to keep the cold air out. I could hear a hoot from an owl outside my window talking to the wind. I never have understood why people thought owls are a sign of danger or evil. I think they are mysterious and I find them seductive in a unique sort of way. I took a quick shower and laid down to rest. I had been having trouble sleeping lately and once again, I found myself tossing and turning, trying to drift off to sleep.

I finally felt myself sinking into what I call dreamland, and then I seemed to awaken and saw her at the foot of my bed. She was shrouded, and seemed more like a shadow or a ghost than a human. In fact, I was certain she wasn't human at all. She seemed to change as the shadows in the room shifted. My eyes would almost focus and then she'd seemingly become invisible and then become a shadow again. She changed right before my very eyes. I don't know how I even knew she was a woman. I just did. She carried with her an air of seductive allure. This nuance seemed to envelop the room and me. Her allure seemed to carry a life force all of its own, and she had a presence that was intriguing and very tantalizing.

I can't explain it, but I found myself becoming sexually aroused suddenly and out of the blue. It felt as though soft and teasing hands were roaming my entire body and all at once. It felt as if these hands could touch everywhere on my body at the same time. It was unlike any human experience I had ever encountered. I could see my body move under the touches, but sometimes I could not see anything visible – just a shadowed ghostly form. I was scared to death yet turned on immensely all at the same time. I felt her hand pulling my cock up and down, but I couldn't see it. It was an invisible action and it looked eerie, but it felt so amazing I didn't care. I couldn't pull myself from her grasp.

Part of my body wanted to escape and run from my house forever; the other part of me felt sexual pleasure like nothing human I had ever felt. I could feel the fingers milking my flesh, I could feel their icy grip squeezing my hot throbbing meat, but there was nothing before me. As I watched my foreskin slowly being pulled up over my cockhead, I wanted to cry out, but all I could do was moan and arch my hips up off the bed. I felt a mouth encircling my cockhead and sucking it as if it had never been nursed before. I felt an invisible tongue licking rings around the ridge, driving me insane with pleasure.

I could feel the icy cold breath meeting the hot moist lips as they sucked fervently at my tumescent head. Icy fingers were cupping my balls. I swore I could hear the echoes of a gasp as my cock felt like it popped out of an invisible mouth into the chilly night air. I could catch glimpses of her form as she shifted in and out of my vision, but most of the time she was an invisible sexual force like nothing imaginable. I do remember seeing ice-blue eyes staring up at me while she nursed the head of my angry cock. This woman in the shadows was taking me on a sexual journey like none other, and I wasn't sure I'd even survive it.

The Eyes of Intensity

Her eyes grew even more intense as she captured me within their stare. I quickly figured out that her power came from behind their steel blue illusion. Her eyes were the answer to why she had a shadowed exterior. They held the secrets of who she was and who she may have been once.

Suddenly without warning, I felt an icy breeze and looked, and she was underneath my body. I felt my cock snaking its way inside of her, although I saw nothing of substance but her ice-blue eyes; everything else was in the form of illusive shadows. Her eyes met with mine and held me within their seductive trance as I slipped deep within a velvet tunnel. It is hard to explain but she was as hot as fire but as cold as ice all at once. It felt almost like a menthol blanket caressing my wanton cock. The feeling was fascinating. The thrill of cold and the comfort of heat embracing my throbbing meat were an experience that blew my mind. I didn't know if this was real, whether I was dreaming, or if I had simply went insane. I heard her speak but her voice sounded like ripples of water beside a brook. It was like sift waves of water that made their way to my ears. Her voice alone was pure sexual enticement, and it enchanted me beyond explanation.

Even though I saw no fleshly body as I reacted to her voice, I could feel her within my arms as I rode her and thrust deep within her fiery yet chilly oasis. It felt like warmed honey on ice inside of her. My cock was neither hot nor cold but a sultry blend of both. I craved more and more and desired to go deeper still. It felt as if I could enter her 10 feet within her shadow. I thrust further and further in, and there seemed to be no end or beginning. I felt as if my body became part of her form. I wondered how any earthly being would ever please me again after this experience. It transcended all things I had ever done.

Her lust floated on the night, a specter of delicious invisibility. I could feel her presence long before I felt her silent fingertips trace my flesh into stiffness. There was no warning or awareness – only the sudden feeling I was not alone. I would lay in bed searching for any indication of her presence or movement that would give me any clue of her essence. When my cock slipped inside her, it felt like stolen demand moistened with the ache of eagerness. When she got on top of me, she rocked on my throbbing manhood and I could almost feel her swollen cunt lips as they greased across my flesh. The night swelled with her demands that settled on my eager flesh. There was no stopping her nor reason to want such. Her moans were echoes of the silence, her breath, and the shadows that flickered the candle beside the bed. Her fingertips traced my nipples with a knowing circle of expectation. I could feel her desperation as her pace increased. It was as if I am in a dream and am the captive beneath the pleasure. I could not see that which held me as prisoner to her touch. I could not hear the sounds of her greedy flesh sucking at my yearning cock. I could not smell the delicious aroma of her slick pussy as it rode my bulging boner. I desired to smell every fevered essence of her, but I couldn't no matter how hard I tried. But she was there; I strained until my eyes hurt to see any evidence of her as she rode my cock to no avail.

She was the shadow that faded in and out of my mind like some will-o'-the-wisp born of enchantment and created in passion. She was the fantasy that many of us have but never get to partake of. I am convinced my mind formed her and she simply came to be for me – and only me. I was special to her. I felt as though it was only me whom she craved and ached for. She drank every inch of my cock inside and her cunt swallowed its hot seed. It seemed as if I came over and over. It was like cumming 20 times in a row at least. At some point, it became like one constant orgasm that I couldn't release my cock from. It was almost painful but still it was molten ecstasy on wings of passion. If I listen close, I can still hear the ripples of her enticing voice in my mind. I was bound and determined to make love to her and fuck her again.

I will never really know if it was real or just my imagination and fantasy. I will never know if I simply desired her into being. I can never forget the electric blue stare of her eyes or the caress of her endless shadow around my wanting body. Her warmth and her iciness are still a mystery to me. How she could be absolute sexual heat and ice-cold winter all at the same time will haunt me forever. I have since tried to get her back but nothing yet. I feel it has to be the perfect set of circumstances to get her to come to my bed. I didn't know what those were, but I know what I felt. I felt almost as if I had fallen deeply in love with her and totally in lust as well. She was the perfect combination of both extremes in life. Her pussy was both gentle and demanding.

Her kisses were innocent and they were greedy too. Her touch was like sparks of flames and tips of icebergs all at once. She could suck my cock and fuck me at the same time. She had power over me now. I don't think I'd ever be free from her passionate hold on me. I don't know if I could stand the pain of not having her much longer. I felt dead inside as I thought about it. Nothing or no one on earth could or would ever come close to what the shadow woman and I shared that night.

I may sound insane and I wonder many times if I am, but I know that it was real – at least to me. I didn't care if I was insane. I'd go insane a million more times to hold her once more. I would give my life to feel her soft shadowy caresses, her icy kisses, and her hot mouth suckling my prick head. I would kill to feel her tongue tip upon my rigid head and rim. I will absolutely never forget those ice-blue eyes. They were the key to her whole mystery. Everything she said, breathed, and did centered around her blue orbs of desire. Her eyes held her beauty, her charm, and her beautiful seductive power. She was the essence of beauty to me; even in her vaporous form, she was gorgeous in my mind. She was my darkest lust and my lightest love all inside of one shadowy woman on an October night. I began to get chills so I got up from writing in my journal, and I heard my friend, the owl, outside my window as I closed out the brisk air. I went to each window and he sang upon the wind louder and louder as if he were right beside me. I latched them each one, a familiar feeling embraced me, and I knew at that moment what it was. Was I dreaming? Was I insane? The owl seemed to answer my questions with a no. He knew the secrets of the shadow. He was telling me what was right there beside me all along.

9 DEAR DIARY

Prologue

I cannot believe what has happened in my life and all because of one hot little sister. I have fallen for my best friend's little sister and I don't know what I am going to do about it, but I am in deep shit! All I have is my journal to talk to because no one can ever find out about my lust for her. I am 23 years old and grown, and she is only 18 years old. I have known her for years, but here recently I began to desire her in a sexual way. I tried to resist her charms, but I had no power over them or her seductive smile and flirty ways.

I had been Jack's best friend since we were adolescents, and I had grown up around his sister Melanie. I knew her when she was a bratty toothless kid, but my oh my, how she has grown up nicely and in all the right places. When Melanie turned 18, it was like her beauty and sex appeal blossomed right before my very eyes. Because I have been a part of their family, it makes me lusting after her taboo and forbidden. Jack and his family would hate me if they knew. Here lately, I have simply tried to stay away from their house, but Jack was always inviting me to do stuff with him. Once invited, I found it impossible to resist going to their house and hanging out.

I have just gotten back from a visit as a matter of fact, and once again, I became obsessed with Melanie to the point I could hardly concentrate on anything else going on around me. She was consuming every corner of my mind and my thoughts. Hell, she was even taking over most of my dreams at night. Tonight, she looked so beautiful and sexy. She had on a white miniskirt and scarlet red tank top. I could see her sexy legs and her pointed nipples through her shirt fabric. It was enough to give me an instant boner in my jeans. My friend Jack kept talking to me, but I swear I never heard a damn word he said. Jack's dad went upstairs to bed and Jack had to go get his mom from work, so that left me there with Melanie. This was a dangerous combination. It seemed to me that Melanie was enjoying teasing me with her smoking hot body.

She made small talk with me and turned me on more with every word that came out of her mouth. There was something about her I could not resist. She looked over at me seated at the dining room table very seductively as if to imply she had a sexy surprise in store for me. I had no idea of just how erotic the surprise she had in store for me was going to be, but I found out very quickly and it was the hottest thing I had ever seen in my life!

The Toy

Melanie quickly ran to her bedroom and came back out. I could tell she had something in her hand behind her back. She put her fingers to her lips as if to say, "Shhhh no talking while I perform my sexual dance for you." I became more enthralled and watched her every move. She lay back onto the sofa and showed me her pink vibrator. My mouth watered in excitement to see her toy her cunt right here in front of me. I couldn't believe I was actually seeing Melanie's luscious cunt. It was not bald, but it wasn't hairy all over either. She had one of those incredibly sexy landing strips that hovered deliciously over the top of her pouty cunt lips. I was getting harder by the second. I stroked my cock over the top of my jeans while Melanie played an orgasmic symphony on her pussy. She moaned in delight in a very sweet and seductive tone that drove my cock wild. I thought I was going to pop off right there in my jeans. She jerked her gorgeous body up and down while she grazed the end of the vibe across her swollen clit. It looked good enough to eat. I so desired to take that hot clit in my mouth and roll it around on my hot hungry tongue.

I pulled my cock from its zippered compartment and stroked it slowly so she could see me while she fingered her pussy. I wanted her to realize how fucking horny she made my hard as steel dick. My head bulged like a purple pulsing plum. The ridge was hard and pronounced as well. Her fingers started flicking as well as the vibe lunging deep within her wanting tunnel. She was damn near beside herself she was so turned on. She was sucking her pointed nubile tit as well and practically growling as she did so. She absolutely was starving for her own tits. It made me shoot a bit of pre-cum watching this lusty display. She was so damn hot and strands of white pussy cum were pouring out of her twat now. She trembled in wanton ecstasy as she started to have a wave of orgasmic pleasure.

She moaned a long animal-like wail and gushed a huge squirt of juice from her cunt. I couldn't believe what I was seeing as the last few gushes pulsed from between her pussiatic pleasures. Just about that time we heard Jack and her mom pulling up in the drive way, I zipped my unwilling and hurting dick up in my jeans real quick and Melanie flew buck naked to her room to get dressed. Jack walked in with a suspicious look on his face and his mom said hello and headed upstairs to bed with his dad. "Is everything okay here dude? You look like you just saw a ghost." "Yeah it's cool," I muttered rubbing my eyes. "Hey bro, I am beat how about I head home. I am bushed." No pun intended of course I thought to myself.

All the way home, I stroked my muscle slow and even until I brought myself to the height of orgasm right there diving in my seat. "Damn what a mess I am going to have to clean up." I thought to myself and headed home to write in my trusty diary/journal. I guess now that I am 23, it is about time I started calling it a journal. I have always been a writer by heart. I loved putting my thoughts and emotions on paper. It helped me to sort out my feelings, but with Melanie, the feelings were all out unadulterated lust. In my eyes that wasn't much to sort out. It was clear as a bell to me. I wanted her, and she wanted me. Something told me we would be doing something about that very soon.

Unstoppable Cravings

All through the rest of the evening, I dreamed about gorgeous Melanie and her pink vibrator of pure lust. Throughout my dreams, she and I came over and over again. We also fucked every which way but loose. We fucked and sucked until we collapsed into a sent heap on her bed. It was a dream of dying and going to heaven. I didn't want to wake up. But when I did, my dick was angry and swollen and just about ready to spew. I took two strokes to it, and I came groaning loudly all over my bed sheets. "Damn another mess I thought!" as I stripped the sheets from my bed and took them to the laundry room. I had to do something about my raging and craving sexual need for my best buddy's little 18-year-old sister. The girl I once called a brat was now the object of every sexual need and desire I had ever had. I knew before this day was over I was going to screw her slow and deep and hard and fast. I just wasn't sure quite how yet, but I would find a way that's for sure.

I thought on and off about it all day until I decided to call Melanie and be bold. I was going to tell her what was on my mind and see if she would agree to see me out somewhere alone. I dialed her number nervously. I could hardly stop my hand from shaking and my heart from pounding in my chest. It was pounding so hard I could hear it.

"Hello," said the voice of my angel on the other end of the line.

"Melanie, hi it's Rob. Remember me your brother's best pal and lifelong friend?"

I said with a laugh and she joined in as well.

"Of course, I remember you silly. What's up?" she said coyly.

If only she knew how funny that was. My cock had grown 2 inches just speaking to her hot ass. "Well would you like to meet for a pizza somewhere and talk?" I asked a bit shyly. "Sure what time?" I told her to meet me at the Pizza Barn in about an hour. I was so fucking excited. I knew I was about to fuck her and nothing anyone could do would stop me now.

When Melanie walked into the Pizza Barn, all eyes turned including mine. She looked hot as fuck in her tight pink mini dress that was sleeveless and showed off her tan beautifully. This girl really rocked my world. We ate some pizza and talked small talk and then we began to talk about our wild tryst the night before. I asked her if she was ready to see what my place was like. I could tell she was getting horny by the way she fidgeted and smiled at me so sweetly yet lustfully.

I unlocked the door and asked her to

make herself at home. I went to the bathroom and fantasized how amazing it would feel to slip between those two carnation pink lips she had. I poured us both a glass of Chablis and it didn't take but a moment before we were all over each other. "Oh Rob fuck me!" she cried in a voice that told me she wanted me to fuck her up against the wall. I took her hands and placed them on the wall behind her head and she draped her right leg around my waist. I started to slide into her juicy cunt and it literally felt like a heated and seductive oven of pure pleasure. I groaned as I slid in and out of her with my hips in a grinding motion that seemed to drive her wild!

"Mmm..." she moaned. "You feel so fucking hot sliding in my starving cunt!"

I could literally smell the aroma of musky sex and her heady pussy upon the air of my living room. The scent of sex drove me insane with fervor. I banged her so hard her ass cheeks were slapping the wall behind her. I lifted her up into my lap and carried her hot body to my bedroom. I told her I wanted it doggie style so she backed her tight ass onto my raging cock. It felt like velvet inside of her love tunnel, and I could hardly hold back my cock squirt any longer. I loved watching her pussy perform its sexual magic from behind. Her pink lips grasped and sucked at my dick like a lollipop. It drove me nuts and I knew soon I was going to shoot my load. I could tell she was about to burst as well. We both reached our orgasm at the same time and we groaned out loud in animal lust as we mingled our cream together in heated ecstasy.

We fucked and sucked for a few more hours and then I drove her back to her place. She French kissed me out in my vehicle and told me she wanted to fuck again real soon. I knew that's what I wanted as well. I also knew that if we kept this pace up we would get caught one day, but right now, all I cared about or even could think about was Melanie and making her cunt feel satisfied. I planned on doing that for as long as she wanted it.

10 LOVE BITE

I had tried all semester to get his attention. Since the first day I saw Evan Murphy at college, I knew he was my true love. I also knew he was the object of the hottest and most delicious desire. I oftentimes lie in my bed at night and masturbate thinking of how he would feel pressed up against my hungry flesh. In my wildest dreams and fantasies, he felt amazing and incredible. In real life, I had a feeling he was even more passionate than that. When love takes its bite out of a person and engages their heart, there is no cure. Once bitten, you are infected with the desire to have that one person, and you will stop at nothing to get their love and their lust.

I had secretly admired Evan from a

distance for months now. It seemed like it had been years. Sometimes, I think a person just knows when they are staring into the face of their destiny. Not only did Evan excite me in this way, he was the object of my most lustful and wanton thoughts and daydreams as well. Every time I slipped into a hot bath or shower, my fingers automatically took a journey between my thighs to my pulsing mound of hair and lips. Every time I fingered off in the tub, I would have racing thoughts about Evan eating my pussy out and how amazingly hot it would feel.

I could imagine his mouth making a trail from my neck straight down to my red swollen labia. I closed my eyes and imagined such a thought, and once again, I found my fingers tracing atrial between my lips. I was seething and drenched inside my hot cunt. I wanted Evan so bad and I truly felt that if I thought about him enough, one day it would happen and I could taste his lips upon mine and feel his flesh pressed to mine.

Destiny Calls

The next day was the best day of my entire life. I did finally see that destiny does come to call if you only dream it. I was in the cafeteria at the university when I heard a man's voice behind me. I turned to look, and it was Evan, my dream lover.

"Excuse me, may I sit down?" Evan asked with a handsome and sexy grin on his face.

"Yes, please do," I answered a bit too eagerly.

He did sit down, and we talked like we had known each forever. Before we knew it, we found ourselves in Evan's apartment enjoying a bottle of white wine together. It truly seemed magical. One moment I was in the shower fingering my cunt dreaming of him, and the next, we were sitting on his sofa with nothing but the air of lust between us smoldering. We knew that at any moment, we would give into the feeling of lust and desire that was swirling around us. I just wondered who would make the first move. It was me. I couldn't hold back any longer. He made me so damn horny I finally reached in, and we began kissing like starved animals.

His kiss was the taste of molten desire upon my lips. His hands roamed over my entire wet and turned on body. He slipped his fingers underneath my skirt. I felt his middle finger slip inside my cunt underneath my mass of bushy hair. I moaned in red-hot pleasure. He went in and out of my furry pussy making it drool with desire to be fucked hard. He slowly added fingers to my cunt. First one and then three, and before I knew it, he had all of them plunging to the depths inside my hot snatch.

I reached over and unzipped him, and his dick sprang out of his zipper like a jack in the box. His head was bulging and red hot. The rim was pronounced and swollen. I circled lightly around it making him squirm and let a bit of pre-cum ooze from his aching cock head. I was in complete shock that I was actually about to make love to and fuck the man of my deepest desires.

Lust and Love

Evan took me by the hand and led me to his bedroom. He laid my body on his bed and began kissing me and devouring my flesh like an animal. We undressed each other vehemently and began to make love, he slipped his cock inside of me inch by delicious inch. I moaned as each inch of his molten cock went inside my horny pussy. I could hardly control the need. I pulled him to me restlessly and kissed him mimicking the way he plunged his sword deep inside my hot tunnel. He place my legs one at a time up by his ears and ground his dick even further inside my swollen pussy. It felt amazing getting fucked by the man I had fantasized about so many times before.

I felt in love and in lust with him all at the same delicious time. He bit and nibbled at my neck flesh as he screwed me hard. I bit his neck back tasting his warm skin underneath my teeth. He tasted like pure unadulterated lust. I badly wanted his face in between my thighs devouring my cunt juice. I asked him to go down on me and he happily obliged.

He lowered his head between my thighs and began tasting my lips one at a time, tempting them to swell bigger than they had ever before. My lips were the most sensitive part of my pussy, and I practically screamed out like a wild animal as he played with them in his mouth. Every nibble and lap was pure ecstasy. He licked and twisted each pink lip and made me squirm in red-hot pleasure. I begged him to tease my clit and make it stand up like a small cock. He did so and it felt fucking amazing. I was dripping in juice. My pussy was drenched front to back, and I had to hold back or I felt I might squirt in his mouth right then and there. I lifted my ass up off the bed towards his hungry mouth. He then began to do quickened tongue flicks upon my hard clit tip. That drove me over the brink of sexual pleasure. I jerked my body upwards even more as he flicked and flicked with his horny tongue. I could smell my musky cunt need infiltrate the room with its essence. The more his tongue did its magic on my clit, the hornier and hotter I became.

He was eating my pussy better than I ever believed was possible. I had many times wished I could eat my own cunt. I had tried to thrust my pussy up to my mouth before, but I had never managed to succeed. I always wondered what my fleshy lips felt like in a mouth. He had fulfilled my desires. I knew I was getting eaten out better than I ever could right then. There was no way I could possibly feel better sexually. I flipped over right before I was about to squirt my pussy off and begged Evan to fuck me doggie style. I loved feeling a set of balls slap my ass as they plunged deeper inside my swollen tunnel of greed.

I could feel his balls slap hard upon my white ass flesh. I could tell they were swollen and just about ready to pop off. They felt as though they were full of white cum. I knew he was craving to shoot his load. I could feel the presence of his seed already inside my cunt. I could almost smell dick cum in the air he was so fucking horny. He slammed his prick harder and harder inside my seething love box.

I pushed backwards towards his greedy cock, and I looked back at him and told him to fuck me hard and cum inside of me. "Fuck me hard Evan fuck me baby fuck me!" I screamed as his intensity grew with every stroke. He felt so damn hot I could hardly hold back my pussy cream. I pushed back towards him with as much force as he banged my hot cunt. I knew that soon both of us would cum. There was no way we wouldn't.

Finally, neither of us could hold back the obvious any longer. It was a race almost to see who would shoot off first. Evan began unloading in me, and I followed about a second behind him, cumming all over his horny cock. He groaned loudly, groped my hips, and dug his fingers into my flesh as he came deep inside of me. He squeezed tightly against my ass as his dick kept squirting off. He had a huge load that shot off inside of me, and it made me feel wonderful all over my body. I also shot off all over him, and my pussy drenched his cock and my cream was all over his cock hair.

After we both came, I desired to taste our mingled juices all over his cock. I looked at him and asked him if he minded if I sucked our juices from his dick. I went down on it, and he began to re-grow a hard boner. I circled his hardened dick rim with my tongue tip, and he groaned in pleasure once more. His dick grew bigger the more I suckled away at the juices that resided on it from our fuck session. I knew I was about to make the man of my dreams squirt once more deep down my throat. I was right. Two more licks and throat of my mouth down on his dick and he got rigid all over and unloaded down my throat. He groaned an animal sounding groan that rocked his whole body.

That first afternoon with Evan was something out of an erotic novel. He satisfied every longing and sexual need I had ever had. Nothing I had ever fantasized even came close to topping what he had done in the flesh. After making love to and fucking Evan, I knew no one would ever be able to satisfy me but him. We shared an intimacy and a sexual bond that was rare. I knew it, and I could feel deep down that Evan did as well. We had been bitten by the ultimate desire. We had met the person who could fill our every sexual and intimate need.

He had not merely fucked me; it was as if he became me. Every move of his cock inside me felt like my body filled to completeness. When he had come inside me, it felt like it was my cum squeezing out inside me. I had never felt so complete in my life. My gasps had been his gasps, my moans his moans. The feeling of his hard cock inside me would haunt me forever and be the measure of every other encounter. I knew in my heart, mind, and body that it was Evan I had to have and that his love bite had taken me over, and I would never be satisfied again until he came within me over and over. I craved him more than ever now. But I knew he would be back. I knew deep within he would. I simply had to conjure his presence and his essence, and he would find me yet again. He would probably walk up when I was least expecting it. He would first come to me in a dream and then in reality. I decided to focus intently on him and see what happened. It didn't take long and once again, I was being bathed in the juices of Evan. In his arms is where I belonged. His arms took me over and covered me in all that I ever wanted or needed forever.

11 MEMORY OF NIGHT

Prologue

I was excited about going on an overnight train ride to up-state New York to visit a close friend. I had always heard that trains were very romantic passenger vehicles, but little did I know just how so until I embarked upon my journey that Friday night at around 7 o'clock. I boarded the train and found my seat #49. I wasn't paying much attention until I took a closer look at my fellow passenger.

I was completely mesmerized. I was aboard this romantic train smack dab between two hot ladies. I don't mean they were kind of hot. I mean they were smoking fucking hot!

Chapter 1: Pleasure Train

As the train pulled out, we started to move along at a nice gentle pace. It was very relaxing. The waitress came and took our orders, and I offered to order these two lovely ladies a soda. The three of us all ordered Dr. Peppers. And both ladies smiled at me sexily. I swear I could feel myself blush. I hope they hadn't noticed. I had a bit of a shy side about me. I had always been especially shy around the fairer sex. There was something about a beautiful girl that made me crazy.

Also, even though I was 20 years old, I was still a virgin. I just noticed also that the three of us were in the far back of the train. I had been so enamored by their looks I had failed to notice. I didn't like telling people I was still a virgin. It didn't make me sound like much of a man. It made me sound like a weakling. But I knew very soon I was going to have sex with a woman. I felt deep inside my ones and my pants.

I was so lost in thought I failed to notice the redheaded girl of the two smiling at me rather seductively. I smiled back my hottest smile of course, and she looked down at my crotch and licked her luscious kips as she did so. I could tell she was horny by the look of seductive need in her green eyes. I wanted her so badly in that moment I could practically taste her pointed nipples that I could see poking through her sheer pink tank top.

I adjusted my now growing boner in my pants to show her what her hot smile and body were doing to my dick in my jeans. She kind of wiggled in her chair, which made me very hot, I must say. I had been around girls enough to know that when they squirmed in their chairs, they were horny and wet usually. I think they were trying to rub their lips on the seat. That is just my personal opinion. I had seen cunts in magazines, and the lips are my favorite part of a hot nasty cunt.

The lips of a pink pussy looked so rubbery and tasty. They looked as though they could be lapped and licked on for hours and drive a woman wild with lust. I wish I could plant my mouth on a cunt right now. My cock was getting more bonerized by the moment. It was all I could do not to pull the fucking dick out and jerk the ever-living cream out of it. But I wasn't quite that brave yet. I noticed the brunette girl was beginning to really watch me and the red head make eyes at each other and turn each other on. She seemed to be getting a bit turned on herself by how she shifted in her chair doing the pussy lip rub, as I like to say it. She had a throw blanket on the train draped over her lap, and she lifted it a bit and gave me a cunt's eye view of her goodies. I can honestly say her goodies were in fine shape. She had a big dark bush that from out of it protruded 4 of the sexiest brown lips I had ever laid eyes upon. I noticed even the saucy red head took a look at the brunette hottie's cookie. She licked her pale pink lips seductively as if she wouldn't mind burying her face in that dark furry package. She sexily recovered her dick hardener, and then all we could see was her hand under the blanket giving her pussy a work over. I could hear the slippery juices but not see. It was amazingly erotic, and the red head started to ease her fingers under her skirt by this time as well.

I couldn't believe my good fortune. Here I was a virgin with a hurting purple boner in my jeans and two hot chicks fingering to my left and to my right. I really thought I had died and shot straight to heaven. I adjusted my woody again in my pants and laid him snakelike on my thigh for the two lovely ladies to see. Now that the sun was totally down, the dim lighting on the train lent a sexy ambience to our back train seats. I knew we were really going to kick up the action a notch or two, three, or four now.

Chapter 2: The Steam Builds

The sexual tension in our back train

seats was growing and building up steam by the second. The faster our train flew down the tracks, the more heated our 3-way seduction became. By what I could see, the little red head was starting to remove her skirt and simply cover herself loosely with a throw as well. I had my eyes fixed on her ivory legs and crotch so that I wouldn't miss a single glimpse of her snatch when she flashed it to me. I didn't either, and I was not disappointed in the view before my eyes. She actually had a redheaded cunt. It is the first time I had ever seen it, but it was here right in my vision and boy what a hot vision it was. It was kind of curly haired and almost copper colored all over her luscious pussy. It was sexy enough to send my cock to outer space before it shot back down to earth.

I looked over to the brunette who was now once again revealing her dark snatch to me and the other hot babe. I knew it was time to show these ladies my cock. I figured the suspense was absolutely killing them. I slowly unzipped my pants to keep them drooling in suspense. They began to finger their pussies more ferociously as I slowly unzipped and let my dick pop free from its hidden cave. It bolted from my zipper like a horse bolted to a race. I stroked my meat up and down slowly so that these two beautiful goddesses would know just how well hung I was. Their eyes widened in fierce and illusive imagination. Their own self-pleasure began to intensify as the three of us roared closer to the height of climax just as out train roared through the tunnels and down the winding tracks. I noticed that the redheaded babe was getting up from her seated position to my left and kneeled down in front of me.

"May I suck your delicious looking cock, baby?" she asked me sweetly and oh so seductively.

I am no fool, so of course I said yes. I was almost overly anxious to have a set of warm lips upon the head and shaft of my throbbing and pulsating cock. She softly began to run the very tip of her greedy tongue up and down the sides of my blue veined member. I shuttered all over my stiff frame from head to toe. My body felt waves of erotic pleasures wash across it like a tidal wave of anticipation. I looked down and saw her head bobbing up and down my wanton shaft slow and then vehemently she would pick up her sucking pace. I wasn't able to hold off and I felt the first drops of pre-cum ooze from the top of my purple head. I groaned softly in obvious agreement and satisfaction with what her amazing mouth was doing to my fascinated cock. It felt as though my cock had taken on a life force all of its own underneath the enchanting spell of her licking, sucking, and lapping.

The beautiful brunette kept watching and toying her hot cunt at the same time. She had a small vibrator thrusting it in and out of her luscious furry pussy while she watched the red head suck me like a vacuum cleaner. I was in paradise with the situation. It was a great way to lose my virginity at least my oral sex virginity. The red head was damn near-balls deep with her mouth sucking the ever-living fuck out of my trouser snake. My body was bucking upwards off of the seat in wanton pleasure. The brunette eased over closer and asked me to finger her twat. I was happy to do so, and I eased one finger inside her hot liquid cunt and then slowly I added fingers until I was damn near fisting her hungry pussy.

She ground down upon my fingers, and I could feel her luscious brown lips grabbing at my fingers tightly as if they would refuse to let go. At the same time, I was getting a mouth treat like no other. She was treating my dick like an amusement park and I felt like the cotton candy she was so eagerly partaking of. I could hardly contain my obvious pleasure at what was taking place. I was smack between a beautiful red head getting ready to drink my load of sweet dick cum and another woman letting me finger her snatch off. I was in heaven, plain and simple.

I could feel the sexual energy aboard our train ignited and increased, and I knew it wouldn't be long before the three of us came in unison. The dark-haired hottie reached down and fingered the red head's snatch, while she continued to suck me hard and ferociously. I bucked harder and harder, and the brunette squirmed atop my hand that was plunging madly inside her wanting cunt. Her lips gripped and grabbed at my fingers while they thrust inside her wet tunnel. I felt my prick stiffen up like a piece of steel. I knew that it was moments from releasing its thick cream down the red head's throat. By the feel of the sucking power of my girl's pussy, I knew she was about to pop off as well. The red head bucked back onto the dark-haired girl's hand hard and furious. Suddenly, it seemed as if the roar of the train's engine pierced through every muscle in my body as I began to cum hard and long. I gritted my teeth and exploded like a bottle rocket down her hot and greedy mouth and throat. I could hear her gulp furiously as I shot one wad after another into her mouth. It was all I could do not to scream out in pure ecstasy.

The two girls both started to shoot their pussies at about the same time. It was smoking hot. The brunette's pussy grasped my fingers like a chokehold and I felt her hot juice start running profusely down my fingers and onto my wrist. When I felt that, I shot another wad into the other girl's mouth, she rose up then with cum dribbling down her chin and squirted all over the other girl's hand. There we were, the three of us, on this pleasure-packed train ride cumming for dear life at the same time. I simply could not picture anything hotter in my mind that this moment in time. I will always have this memory of that hot night burned into my mind. It was the single most erotic night of my life, and I had a feeling I'd never again experience anything close to what that night on the train was like.

12 THE MYSTERIOUS LOVER

For as long as I could remember, I was a loner and always yearned for love, passion, and all that comes along with it. Known only as the stuck-up business executive, little do they know, I worked hard every day and would go home to the same routine. I had no glamorous life, no close personal friends, no relationship, and definitely no sex life. I was often envious of coworkers who would discuss the great sex and the men in their lives. Lately, I began to wonder if I would ever find a lover who could fill the black hole in my life and satisfy me. It all started the day that I received a dozen red roses to my office; in that card, it said one word, "Yours."

It was a long day at work, and I was finally able to relax after a stressful day of meetings. It was later than normal after I left the office and it was dark out. I was walking home to the same place that I'd lived for the past three years with the night breeze calm and blowing against my skin. Like before, there was this strange feeling against my skin as if I was being caressed, and it brought me such longing thoughts. Just like clockwork, I started thinking deeply how it felt to be deeply loved and comforted by someone's touch. I continued to walk, and I welcomed the comfort from the night air as it caressed my skin. My heartbeat began to race as I felt the air seep in between my breasts.

I could only hear my own footsteps, but there was a strange feeling as I continued to walk that someone was walking behind me. I stopped on full alert to turn around, but to no surprise, I was alone. I picked up my pace walking further into the secluded area past several trees. Then I finally heard a sound coming from behind me. I looked back only to find standing right behind me the most handsome man I've ever laid my eyes on. As I stared, I was quick to notice that he was missing his clothes and completely naked. It wasn't hard to miss his beautiful ripped chest, muscular shoulders and arms. As my eyes roamed up his body, I took in the rest of his features: smooth skin, green eyes, tall, dark hair, and sexiest smile that I've ever seen. This was a beautiful man that I could only dream about.

As I continued to stare at him, before I could have a chance to speak, he grabbed my waist and pulled me to him. Our bodies pressed against each other so tightly that I tried to pull back from his embrace and resist his unexpected seduction. The more I tried to pull away and resist him, the more that I wanted to find out about this mysterious beautiful man. Loving his attention and tight embrace overpowered my better judgment; I simply didn't mind, I wanted him.

This sensation was strange, yet familiar because I had always longed to have the feeling of comfort and love. We stared into each other's eyes with lust and passion, as if no one else in this world existed. We both tightened our embrace and begin to kiss passionately as if we were long-lost lovers reuniting. He backed me farther out of view into one of the tall dark trees and resumed kissing me passionately all over. His lips gently kissed my bare skin as he removed my clothes piece by piece until I was completely naked before him.

I moaned softly and arched my back against the tree as he kneeled and found my dripping pussy fully bare to him. His tongue found my clit and began to lick my juices as if it was his last meal. The need in his eyes, and he looked up ensured me that this was no dream and that this was really happening right here, right now. My pussy became wetter as he continued to lick and suck me into his mouth, holding one of my legs over his shoulder to keep my pussy open wider to him. I was lost at the sensation, and it did not take long for me to cum hard covering my mouth to keep from screaming. He continued fucking my pussy with his tongue, and as I looked down, I found my beautiful stranger fully erect.

Weak from my orgasm, but not yet satisfied, I quickly removed my leg from his shoulder and pulled him to stand. Breathing hard, I looked deep into his eyes; I knew that I wanted to please him too. I let my fingers wander down his smooth, muscular chest until I found his hard erection that throbbed against stomach. I grabbed on to his long hard cock and began to stroke it wondering if it would fit inside my needy pussy or my mouth.

Stroking his cock with my hand just inches from my face, I wanted to return the favor and taste him as well. I leaned over to take the head of his engorged cock into my mouth. He hissed at the sensation. I began slowly with my tongue as I licked up and down from the head to his balls. I took him into my mouth fully, sucking and bobbing up and down almost gagging, but I enjoyed it and so did this mysterious beautiful man who had just pleasured me. I was ready to feel his hard cock cum inside me instead of my mouth, so I gave him one hard long hard suck before I plucked him out of my mouth with a pop. I smiled up at him; I motioned him to lie down with me.

He continued to watch me with longing as I began to slide down to the ground on my back pulling him with me, giving him permission to take me. Without reservation, I began to open my legs wide as I could, offering my wet pussy once again to this beautiful man that just brought me pleasure.

I felt such a connection to him as his gentle hands touched and caressed my skin; it was as if my body was familiar to him. He worshiped my body as he lay down on top of me kissing my neck, my shoulders, and my breasts lovingly. My body began to shake and tremble with need because I wanted to feel his cock inside me. He took his time as if he was memorizing every part of my body, as if he was delaying our impending union.

I grabbed his shoulders and moved my fingers through his hair guiding him to my mouth for another kiss. I felt him slide between my thighs slowly entering my hot awaiting pussy as our kiss as deepened; he filled me to the hilt. I'd never had such a long hard cock fill me with such sensation that wasn't one of the plastic toys whenever I was horny enough to use it.

I couldn't believe what was happening to me, this beautiful man making me feel so much pleasure is something I only longed for and dreamed about. He was initially so passionate and affectionate; however, our lovemaking turned hard and fast as if we both couldn't get enough. He looked into my eyes, holding me tightly as he pumped faster and harder. My breath quickened as I held on to him tighter trying to meet his every thrust. I arched my back and he took one of my nipples into his mouth and sucked hard thrusting harder and harder. I gasped at all the pleasure, and I began to cum milking his hard as steel cock as he continued ramming me over and over.

Before I could calm from the high of the second orgasm, he quickly pulled out, flipped me over to my stomach pulling me to my knees, and without warning, quickly entered me from behind fast and hard. I opened myself to him and welcomed the intrusion as his grasp on my waist tightened to pull me deeper onto his cock. Sweat dripped from our bodies; I moaned louder because the sensation was too overwhelming. I pushed at the tree trunk in front of me for support to keep my head from hitting the tree while he continued fucking me relentlessly. All I could hear was the night air, our heavy breaths, and sweaty skin slapping together as he continued to thrust deeper and deeper. Time seemed to go on and I didn't want him to stop.

His grip on my waist started to loosen up as his hands began to trail from my ass and lovingly up my lower back and shoulders. Leaning down, he kissed the back of my shoulder and neck, while gently cupping my breasts in both hands. He slowly brought me to him with my back against his chest and I turned my head to kiss his lips. It was even more sensual, and he began to slow his movements inside me as our kiss deepened only to look in his eyes and see so much need in this beautiful man.

He indeed needed more because he flipped me onto my back once again entered me hard and fast. My breasts bounced wildly as he pounded into me taking my hard nipples into his mouth licking and swirling his hot wet tongue. This was it; I couldn't take any more of this pleasure and I started to orgasm again for the third time.

It didn't take long before I heard a soft moan and felt him spill deep inside as he kissed my lips hard. Unexpectedly, the beautiful man lifted his head to the sky grunting softly. He brought his head back down to me breathing heavily and we looked at each other basking in our pleasure. He smiled that beautiful smile when I first laid my eyes upon him. Deliciously satisfied, I closed my eyes for a split second and opened them only to realize I was in my bed completely naked and alone.

It startled me because I surely had not imagined this beautiful man and newfound pleasure. I looked around and found no sign of him, the man that had just given me three orgasms and more pleasure than I could've only imagined. I quickly checked my front door only to find that it was locked. Though my mind was blank, there was no sign of the man who I had sex with the night before. I didn't even recall coming home from work, though I definitely had an aching body. Looking in the mirror, I saw in delight the handprints left on my waist from the beautiful man's tight grasp as he fucked me from behind, this was certainly no dream. I was filled with enough memory to replay the previous night events, as I got ready for work.

After work that day, I came home normally to the same routine; had my dinner and took a long hot bath. Lying on the bed looking up at the ceiling, my mind wandered to last night with thoughts of the mysterious beautiful man. I asked myself if I could've been dreaming, though it seemed so real and my body felt unusually satisfied.

The next morning I awaken to find myself completely naked with an achingly satisfied feeling between my legs once again. I slowly moved my fingers between my thighs finding my pussy still hot and dripping wet. I was surprised to find a load of semen and pussy juice inside me, and I smelled like sex.

It began to happen over and over again. The first several nights after the encounter, I was sure that I dreamed making love to this mysterious beautiful man every night. One night, I awakened in the dark to find him touching and caressing my body. I remembered that I fell asleep against my body pillow, but once again I loved his presence and my body felt like fire. I could feel him; his need and I know it was him gently licking my erect nipples with his wet tongue.

His expert hands began to stroke my body exactly how I liked it. My beautiful man knew exactly what my body wanted and how I needed it. He made love to my body for the rest of the night loving me from head to toe. He couldn't get enough for me and I couldn't get enough of him, he sent me over the edge completely satisfied from multiple orgasms.

When morning came, my body felt sore and used however nothing same as before. I found that I was fully clothed in my nightgown, the doors and windows locked and bed sheets in place as the night before. However, I knew this wasn't just a dream because once again I smelled like sex and could feel the mix of cum from another night of lovemaking.

Confused, I wanted to enjoy him even if he was just a dream, but the sane side of my mind told me there's more to my mysterious lover.

The workday was less stressful and I was able to get through the day without having thoughts of canceling business meetings scheduled for weeks. I actually enjoyed work today and was able to focus a lot more, though I still had constant thoughts about my mysterious lover. The small ache that I felt was a reminder that he'd been inside me, as if he was still there. My pussy began to get wet all over again as my mind wandered, but just as comfortable as ever.

I went home later that evening to my usual schedule and made myself dinner, checked e-mail and flipped through the television channels until I found something worthy to watch. However, tonight was different because I had such a weird an anxious feeling. I decided to turn in early for the night and took a shower leaving myself completely naked instead of dressing in the usual nightie. Sleeping nude was far from norm for me, however switching off the lights I didn't question myself.

As I lie awake waiting for him, my mind began to wander about my workday, my boring personal life and the mysterious lover who came to me at night. Suddenly, a movement across the room and the sight of a silhouette startled me. My heartbeat began to race; my mysterious lover was here and I was both nervous and excited. I knew it was him because I could feel the air caress my skin as our previous encounters.

I thought that I could be dreaming because so many questions entered my mind. Was my mysterious beautiful man even real? Where did he come from? Had he been in my home all night watching? All of these questions would have to go unanswered because I wanted him dream or no dream.

As my mysterious lover slowly approached the bed, I lie there frozen listening only to the sounds of my heartbeat. I felt the bed shift and I began to unconsciously spread my legs for him smelling the aroma of my wet pussy fill the room. I reached out to touch him just to make sure that he was real and found that he was once again completely naked. It wasn't hard to miss that his cock was already hard as a rock.

The closer that he came, the more my skin tingled. It was the same tender touches and caresses as our first encounter, my need increased for him. I started to feel his hands touch my legs slowly rising to my thighs gently caressing and he moved up further to my bare dripping pussy.

I began to tremble as I felt two fingers enter my slick pussy with slow movements in and out, testing my tolerance. Yes, my pussy was still aching from our previous encounters, but I had waited for him all night and wanted to feel more than his fingers. I had been dreaming of his hard cock all day. As if he heard my thoughts, he removed his fingers from my hot pussy and started to move closer to line his body up with mine. He gently lay on top of me, while adjusting his body between my spread thighs. He hovered over to brush my lips with his, but stopped short and instead felt his breath as he moved across my cheek and ear.

He whispered softly in my ear, "I need you."

I never heard my lover speak any words during our encounters. He only smiled that beautiful smile, grunted and moaned from his pleasure of being inside me.

Tonight was so much different from the other times he'd come to me. I watched the mysterious lover movements as he continued brush his lips across my face lovingly as if he missed me. I savored the moment realizing he was all I wanted in a lover. I still couldn't see his face, only the outline of his strong jaw as he continued to caress my cheeks, my nose, my ears as if he was memorizing every part of me.

There was absolutely no fear inside me, though he definitely had a strong hold on me. When in his presence, he controlled and owned my body. Deep inside, I knew my mysterious lover would not harm me, only bring me pleasure.

I trembled as the tingles ran through my body; he continued to kiss tenderly from my jaw up to my ear and gently sucking my ear lobe into his mouth. It was glorious and I started to moan loudly at the sensations.

He moved to the opposite ear and whispered again, "Let me inside."

I felt the hard ripples of his body across mine and reached with both hands to hold his face to mine. I needed to see his beautiful face again, to see in his eyes if his need mimicked my own desire. As the faint light outside glimmered through the blinds, I caught a glimpse of his face; it was just as I remembered. He peered into my eyes with lust and as if his only goal was to satisfy my need and desire for him.

With all my fears and questions far behind, I basked in his tender touches and attention he continued to give my body. It's as if he was burning the feel of my face into memory. My lover continued to kiss my entire face, leaving wisps of hot breath across my nose, eyes, and chin across to my neck. To give him better access, I arched and turned my neck while I brought my hands to thread his soft locks of hair that tickled my face. He smelled manly, like spice and the fresh night air as his aroma invaded my senses.

There was no thinking at all; my body just reacted to him as the room filled with moans of pleasure as he licked at my skin leaving wet traces from his tongue all down my body. He reached my breasts and began gently rolling my erect nipples between his fingers. He then took my left nipple in his mouth and licking hard, then my right. He continued lower kissing my stomach until he reached my aching pussy.

I could feel his hot breath hovering over my wet pussy and he started to lick my slit slowly before his tongue dove deeper into my wet folds tasting me once again. It was heaven and my moans turned into soft screams of pleasure. His skilled tongue was lapping and licking at my clit as his grasp on my thighs increased.

"Take all of me!" I gasped.

My lover looked up into my eyes letting his tongue make one last lick up my pussy. He started to kiss his way back up my body finally meeting my lips. He kissed my lips hungrily and I opened my mouth to welcome and deepen the kiss. I moaned again, I loved the scent of myself on his tongue and it only increased my need to feel him inside me.

As if he heard my thoughts, he whispered. "Do you need me?"

I couldn't help but moan again in answer.

He grinned cunningly, "Then you'll have me."

There was a small light from the blinds that spread across his face big enough to see the passion in his eyes and deep into his soul. Tonight I knew that I was not only giving him my body once again, but my heart in full. Everything he did to me gave me feeling of protection and satisfaction. His breath began to quicken as he took my lips to his mouth again while grabbing my thighs to give him better access. I wrapped my legs tightly around his waist anticipating his next move.

I whispered to my lover, "Please, I need you now." There was a look of pure passion spread across his face as he pushed gently inside me to the hilt. I grabbed his shoulders as he started to move in and out of me too slow. I proceeded to move with him, giving him all that strength I had to meet his every thrust, hoping he'd pick up the pace.

"Yes," my lover whispered softly above my lips. "I'm here to give you what you need."

Feeling the sincerity of his spoken words, as I looked into his eyes, I whispered, "Please don't leave me. I need you always and forever." Our breathing began to pick up as something changed in the air between us at that moment.

He continued to impale my wet pussy while holding me close to him. I met his every thrust giving everything I had in me to him. This wasn't enough; I wanted him deeper and harder inside my wet pussy filing me, stretching me. It was as if I got some newfound strength because I rolled us so I was on top, without any objections from him.

He was still hard inside me as I began to bounce up and down on his cock as hard as I could. I wanted to show him how much he pleased me, as much as I wanted to please him. I leaned down to kiss him on his lips riding him harder and harder. My lover grabbed my hips as he angled to thrust up harder to meet my soaking pussy.

The sounds of our moans and the slapping of our wet skin was enough to send me over the edge. I came hard, feeling my juices flow out while his pace quickened hammering my pussy over and over. Before I knew it, I was on my knees and he was entering me from behind. I grabbed onto the headboard for leverage because he was giving me what I wanted as if he'd read my mind. I wanted him to fuck me hard and rough. I wanted a reminder the next morning that he had been inside me.

My lover was so deep inside me, that I could feel his balls grinding and smacking against my bare pussy. It felt like hours as my lover fucked me again and again from behind and I loved it. Though I would love to see his face, I think it was his favorite position too because he was so deep in this position, like he was home.

I felt his cock start to swell and grow harder inside me as he grabbed onto my shoulders and pounded faster and harder, the sounds of wet bodies smacking and moaning was such a turn on that it sent me over the edge every time. I pushed back into him as I started to cum milking his hard cock for the second time and pleading with him not to stop only to fuck me harder.

He grunted and trembled with one final thrust and filled my soaking cunt with his cum, deep inside me. I was spent and I froze in place, taking all he had to give me.

He pulled out and flipped us to face one another, his hot breath on my face entrancing me. He whispered, "I won't ever leave you. I'll be here whenever you need me." He moved the sweaty hair that covered my face so he could see me and kissed me gingerly, so sweetly.

We continued to kiss and hold each other close, gentle touches as if to memorize each other's body. I loved his taste, the feel of his body and his kisses were like fresh air. I fitted perfectly into his arms as I began to drift off to sleep.

Later I woke up to soft kisses to my neck and back as my back lie against my lover's front. I felt his hard cock against my back thrusting slightly. I groaned at the sensations of waking up to another round of lovemaking. I arched my back into him turning my neck to kiss his lips. He lifted my leg over his to spread my legs wider and entered my still soaked pussy as our kiss deepened. His movements were deep, yet slow as he made slow love to me. He reached for my breasts fondling them and slowly moved to my clit increasing my pleasure.

"Whenever you need me, I'll be here," he whispered in my ear as we both came as our soft moans and groans filled the room.

I felt completely satiated and satisfied

as I awoke the next morning, alone as usual to a single red rose. I knew that my lover was truthful that he'd be here if I need him, to give me pleasure and fulfill my every need. We are a part of each other now and he's there for me when I desire him each and every night.

AUTHOR'S NOTE

Readers: We want to expand a few of the stories to see where the characters can be explored further. If there are any of the stories that you would like to read more about again, we'd love to hear from you!

Visit our blog at
http://www.jullesmunsen.com
http://www.blancacranston.com/

Join our newsletter for free exclusive previews
http://www.jullesmunsen.com/in
http://www.blancacranston.com/in

Follow us on Twitter at
http://www.twitter.com/jullesmunsen
http://www.twitter.com/blancacranston

Like our page on Facebook at
http://www.facebook.com/jullesmunsen
http://www.facebook.com/blancacranston

Discover our books at major ebook retailers everywhere.